THE SPIDER:
SLAVES OF THE MURDER SYNDICATE

THE SPIDER

MASTER OF MEN!

SLAVES OF THE MURDER SYNDICATE

By Grant Stockbridge

STEEGER BOOKS • 2020

CHAPTER 1
THE FEATHERED DART

RICHARD WENTWORTH whirled the corner, goaded himself to a sprint and ducked into the first darkened doorway. There he crouched, blackjack balanced on his palm. He would make an end, now and for all, of the surveillance which, for a week, had hounded him through the slattern streets of the Underworld. Time and again he had eluded these stealthy shadows, only to have them reappear upon his trail....

A man walked briskly around the corner and, keeping to the curb, came whistling along the street. He was beyond reach of the blackjack, playing the usual cautious game. Wentworth's lips pressed hard against his teeth. He would chance an attack anyway. Damn it, how had they run him down again?

Wentworth was still in hiding, his face quite altered by a half-dozen tiny, puckering scars which a ricocheting bullet had inflicted. All the world, save only two persons, thought him dead, and neither of those two would talk....

The shadower was almost opposite the doorway, and Wentworth hefted the blackjack, tensed ready legs beneath him—but he did not strike. At the moment when he would have sprung forth, he caught the sound of approaching footsteps, ponderous and slow. Only one type of pavement-pounder walked like that—the police.

Wentworth shook his head. He pocketed the blackjack and

slipped out another implement—a thin, hooked probe of surgical steel. It was the work of moments only to unfasten the door behind him with the lock-pick, to fasten it again when he had entered. For the present, he would be free of pursuit. Before they could pick up the trail again....

Through the dark, close cold of the hallway, Wentworth sped; then down into the basement and out into the yard behind the tenement building. The rooms where he lived were only a few blocks away. If he could reach them before his shadow... They

Wentworth leaped with down-swinging sword straight for the black-hooded figure!

would know where he was going, of course, and would hasten there to find his trail again, but perhaps he could gather tools and clothing and escape....

Wentworth cursed bitterly as he sped through the tenement that backed on the one whose door he had unlocked. A few months ago—a few weeks even—this surveillance would have presented no difficulties. He simply would have left his quarters and all that they contained, found new rooms, bought new supplies. But now he was almost without funds; his entire estate, which he had willed to his sweetheart, Nita van Sloan, had been confiscated under the crooked regime of Senator Hoey. Hoey was dead now by Wentworth's own hand, but how could Wentworth, supposed also to be dead, fight for the recovery of the millions which also were lawfully his? If he dared to come to life, he would have to face a mountain of evidence which would prove past any doubting that he was that dread killer of the night, the Spider!

Yes, Wentworth was a murderer in the eyes of the law—a butcher who had slain a hundred, a thousand of his fellow men. They took no account of the fact he killed only those who richly deserved to die, that he alone had prevented a score of master criminals from overwhelming the forces of law and order. And because he had fought so valiantly, the denizens of the Underworld also would rejoice to lay him low. Small wonder then that this ceaseless surveillance harassed him!

AT THE door of the tenement through which he was making his escape, Wentworth hesitated a moment, scanning the darkening street. There was only one person in sight, a young woman who hurried along with her head bent into the sweep of the January wind. Wentworth slipped out and merged into the shadows, but for all his careful concealment, he moved very swiftly. He overtook the girl, was just passing her when an automobile whirled around the corner ahead. Wentworth dodged instantly deeper into the shadows, found the breech of an alley which led between two buildings and stood there tensely, waiting. Of course, this auto might have nothing to do with the men who followed him… Damn, the car was slowing!

Even as Wentworth whirled in flight, he realized that the car was stopping, not at the alley where he crouched, but beside the girl. She realized this at almost the same moment and her head came up; fright stiffened her body. Before she could decide what to do, two men swung out of the car and converged upon her. She screamed, then, whirled to run, but she was too late. The men were upon her.

Tense in his concealment, Wentworth hesitated. This was no battle of his, and a moment's delay in his swift flight might mean all the difference between life and death. Unless he reached his rooms before the men who followed him… Wentworth's lips twisted in a wry smile. A man who thought first of himself would never have become the Spider, would never have sacrificed all happiness and normal life to the service of an ungrateful people. He could not weaken now, even when life itself might well hang in the balance. The two men closed on the girl, whirled her about, and Wentworth stepped from the alley….

"Just a minute, gentlemen," he said suavely.

"On your way, buddy," one of the men snarled. "On your way before you get hurt!"

Wentworth moved closer. He had not drawn the twin revolvers that nestled in armpit holsters. If he needed them, he could snatch them free and shoot within scant fractions of a second. His overcoat was unbuttoned, whipping in the wind….

"Do you really think I'd be hurt?" he asked casually. "Madame, at your service."

One of the men cursed, left the girl's side and came striding toward Wentworth. He had broad, rolling shoulders, a pugnacious jaw, "Listen, buddy...!"

Wentworth struck with the speed of light. His left jolted to the man's face, tilted back on his head; his right fist came up with perfect timing and the thug sprawled senseless to the pavement.

"Now, my good fellow," said Wentworth to the other man. The thug freed the girl and she stood where he left her, swaying a little on her feet, head hanging without strength. The thug had a gun in his hand, but Wentworth saw at once that it was not the usual type of weapon... With the recognition of that fact, Wentworth whipped his hat from his head and shielded his face. His action was almost instinctive—as swift as the reflex of a leg when the knee-cap is tapped. Even so, it was barely in time. There was a subdued, metallic concussion and something plucked at the hat.

INSTANTLY, WENTWORTH was in action. The man leaped back, cocking the queer pistol. He was too far away to reach—and already he was leveling the weapon again!

Wentworth dropped to a crouch and with the almost magical speed of which he was capable, whipped out one revolver and fired. He did not kill the man. The Spider was no wanton slaughterer, and as yet he did not know that these men deserved to die. He smashed the man's right arm, and the thug, with queer, shrill cries, turned and raced up the street, ignoring the car parked at the curb, making crazy, staggering movements as he reeled away. Wentworth rose smoothly to his feet, a movement he accomplished by merely straightening his legs, and crossed to the girl's side. The gun was already back in its holster.

"Is there anything I can do for you?" he asked gently. "Those men won't harm you again, and...."

Wentworth realized abruptly that the girl did not hear him, was not conscious of his presence. He put a hand under her chin, lifted her head and a curse ripped from his throat. There, piercing her left cheek, was a tiny toy-like dart with bright-colored feathers on its end. Wentworth snatched the thing out of her flesh, groped for a handkerchief... The girl swayed; her head came up convulsively and her face twisted, the muscles about her mouth and eyes quivering. The trembling communicated itself to her entire body and abruptly she spun away from Wentworth and began to run in crazy, tight circles, her feet moving with spasmodic quickness. She lifted on her tiptoes and with her arms thrown wide, whirled like a dervish!

Wentworth's eyes widened in horror and shocked surprise. He leaped forward, caught the girl's shoulders and tried to quiet her, but even beneath his firm grip, she shivered and jumped, bounced up and down on her toes, tried to whirl, to run in those crazy circles. And all the while, screams that were hoarse, unnatural and terrifying poured from her mouth.

"Stop it!" Wentworth shouted at her. "Stop it! You're all right now. All right, I tell you!" He slapped her cheeks sharply, but it had no effect, and the moment he released his hold, she began to whirl and whirl again.

"That's not hysteria," Wentworth thought and realized he had spoken the words aloud. He glanced at the dart which he

Richard Wentworth

had dropped to the pavement and a sharp curse pulled his lips back from his teeth. He turned from the madly whirling girl. The man he had wounded was out of sight, but the other still lay supine upon the ground. Perhaps he could be made to explain. Wentworth started toward him, heard a police whistle burble frantically at the corner, and heavy feet beat along the pavement.

In two quick movements Wentworth snatched his hat from

the ground and caught the girl about the waist. He sprang to the car which, gangster-style, had been left with its motor running. Behind him the whistle shrilled, the policeman shouted a hoarse order. As Wentworth sent the car leaping forward, a revolver spoke. The Spider's lips were set in a harsh curve. On the seat behind him, the girl scrambled about, screaming, screaming... Gone now were all thoughts of escape. He must get her to a hospital—and quickly. Heaven alone knew what fearful drug or poison had been injected into her veins through the agency of that dart....

THE AUTO rocked around a corner on screaming tires and the police whistle and banging gun faded away behind him. Wentworth veered around another corner, straightening out for the East Side and Bellevue Hospital... And he realized that the screaming behind him had ceased, that the girl no longer moved around with her convulsive quivering. Wentworth twisted about. She was sprawled, half on the floor, half on the seat, her head lolling limply....

Wentworth slammed on brakes, leaned over the back to touch

the girts throat-pulse with a swiftly bared hand. There was no throb of blood there. He got out of the car, climbed into the tonneau and put his ear to her breast, bared an eyeball with a skillful finger… Then he straightened slowly. There could be no doubt about it. The girl was dead… Snatched from her hurrying walk homeward after a day's work at the office to be tortured by the fearful convulsions of that dancing death… A curse rasped in Wentworth's throat. And what was the purpose of it all?

He heard a police siren nearby, whirled and strode rapidly off along the street. Police were hard on the trail of the car with the screaming woman passenger. The Spider, though innocent, could not delay… His mind was tortured by a thousand doubts as he stole along, once more pressed close against the shadowy buildings for protection. There was little hope now that he could reach his rooms and escape before his pursuers took the trail again. But that was a minor worry. What was the meaning behind this ruthless and public attack—this strange dart that made people dance to their death? He snatched off his hat, hoping the dart he had blocked might have been caught, but it was gone. Heaven grant that this was not the weapon of some new and vaunting madman come to vent his spleen upon the people of the city and gain wealth by murder! Almost always, these geniuses of crime developed some new weapon, some horrible means of killing with which to speed their mad dreams of power and wealth….

Wentworth hesitated across the street from the tenement in which he had rooms, scanning the dark doorway. Impossible, of course, to tell whether men lay in wait for him there… His shoulders set and his hand moved deftly to the revolver

beneath his left arm. Then he crossed the street swiftly, dodged through the door... The hallway was empty, and he went with long, springing strides up the stairs to his door on the second floor back Before he fitted his key to the lock, he felt along the crack at the door's top, and his face tightened ominously. The seal of chewing gum which he had set over the crack had been broken. His room had been entered in his absence! But it might mean more than that. There might be men waiting for him inside now, a death trap....

WENTWORTH KEPT his door-lock well oiled, and the bolt slid from its socket without a sound. He twisted the knob, then hurled the door inward, sprang through the opening at an angle and crouched against the wall with his revolver in his hand.

"Move and you die," he announced coldly, words clipping out between his teeth.

Gun and eyes were focused on the window, a shadow that moved slightly as if someone swayed gently forward and back in the rocking chair. Wentworth drew a small flashlight from his pocket, spewed its widely diffused ray across the room. He came to his feet.

"Nita!" he cried. "Nita, darling, you shouldn't have come here."

Nita van Sloan rose out of the chair with the slow grace which always characterized her movements. Her violet eyes were tender, her lips smiling as she lifted them to Wentworth's hungry caress.

"I had to come, Dick," she whispered.

Wentworth gripped her shoulders hard, shook her a little. Then he whirled across the room, locked the door, flicked on a shaded light before he went back to Nita.

"There isn't even time to talk," he said harshly. "I'm being followed, and I've got to get out of here."

He snatched a suitcase from under the bed, began to dump clothing into it. He stooped to a piece of baseboard. There was a click of a released spring, and an opening was revealed. From it, Wentworth scraped tools and more clothing, a long, black cape and a broad-brimmed hat which would have labeled him before all the world as the Spider.

Nita stood by the window watching, keeping out of the way because she could not help. She did not even bother him with questions. There would be time for that later, now that they were together again. She crossed to the door and stood there, listening. Wentworth's eyes went to her now and again, as he moved with swift, efficient strides about the room. Two months ago she had taken a bullet meant for him, and her gracious body was still weakened by the long, almost losing battle against death. Nita felt his eyes and smiled….

Minutes later, Wentworth flicked out the light, raised the window noiselessly. Nita crossed to his side and together they climbed out upon the low roof which slanted away beneath the window. They crossed it, dropped to the ground and stole away. There was no alley, but Wentworth found a board in the fence which he had loosened and hinged one night. He went through first and the brilliant beam of a flashlight dazzled him. A man's voice rasped out:

"Just stand there a minute, my friend. Tell your buddy to come on through behind you."

CHAPTER 2
BETRAYED!

WENTWORTH HESITATED in the fence opening, eyes blinded. He was stalling for time, hoping that Nita could get away. There was no way of telling who it was who held him thus at gun point, but police or criminal, it made little difference. Capture by either meant death for the Spider.

"Who in the hell are you?" he snarled.

He was conscious of Nita's hand groping in his pocket, withdrawing his blackjack He could not prevent it without betraying her activity.

"Quit stalling," snapped the man. "Come out of that and get your hands up."

Wentworth dropped his suitcase, snarled a curse as it landed on his toe and thus gained a few more seconds. He lifted his hands slowly, stumbled through the fence....

It happened with the sharpness of a shot. The light wavered and fell; the man gasped with pain. Wentworth went toward him in a low, long, headfirst dive. His arms encircled legs, slammed the man flat to the ground... There was no resistance, no movement in the body. Wentworth got hold of the light and picked up his blackjack from the ground.

"A good throw, Nita," he praised quietly. "You got him in the temple with the blackjack"

Nita was beside him, breathing a little quickly, while Wentworth made a swift search of the man's pockets. There was nothing in them to indicate his identity or the purpose of his activities. Wentworth took his gun, recovered his suitcase, and threw an arm about Nita's waist as they went swiftly through the darkness toward the tenement house which reared its black bulk ahead of them. He squeezed Nita.

"They almost had me that time, sweetheart," he whispered. "You always show up just in time."

She laughed uncertainly. There was almost a sob in her breath. Must she and Dick always meet in the midst of death and peril? Must their love always be a sterile battling for the happiness of others? Oh, Dick was a great and a good man. She could have only reverence for his ceaseless fighting for humanity, his untiring pursuit of the enemies of justice who arose now and again from the filthy warrens of the Underworld. But how long was it to continue?

Nita stumbled and Wentworth's strong arm about her waist steadied her. They went a half-dozen blocks at a stiff pace, then found a taxi. Once inside, she sagged against Wentworth's shoulders.

"Guess I'm not… as strong as I thought," she panted.

"Poor child," Wentworth whispered. "Why must you do it, darling? I've begged you not to tangle in my troubles…" His voice died. He knew her strong loyalty, her untiring devotion. It was pain to him, too, that their life could hold no more than this. But how could a man marry the woman he loved, have a home and children when death and disgrace hourly reached out a skeleton hand for his shoulders? It was not fair to Nita, but Heaven knew both of them had fought against a love they had known must prove fruitless. It had been too strong for them....

"Tell me now why you came," Wentworth said gently. "If you had put a notice in the papers, I would have come to you." NITA SHOOK her head, pushed herself erect. She was breathing more easily, though the tremors of her weakness still shook her. She had not fully recovered from her old wound. "My home is watched," she said. "You must never come there."

"Watched by whom?" Wentworth demanded sharply.

Nita shook her head. "Who is watching *you*, Dick?"

Wentworth frowned. "Kirkpatrick, perhaps?"

Stanley Kirkpatrick was his friend, but he was also Commissioner of Police. He was the second person who knew that Richard Wentworth, the Spider, was alive. But there were reasons why he would not talk. Wentworth had put him back in office when his enemies had triumphed over him. They had fought side by side to put down criminals who had a death grip on the city. Even as he spoke, Wentworth did not believe that Kirkpatrick would send men to track down a friend, although he would do even that if he felt that duty demanded it.

Nita said, "No. It's not Stanley. I came to bring you a message from him."

The taxi stopped at an uptown subway station. Wentworth

paid the driver and they went into the kiosk, down the drafty steps. They rode uptown, changed to a downtown train, emerged and took another taxi to a hotel where they registered under false names. Hateful that they could have no other sanctuary than this. In the room, Wentworth made Nita lie down.

"Rest a while, sweetheart," he told her. "Then you can tell me all about it."

He sat beside her, stroking her forehead with long, firm movements of his muscular hands. He stared straight before him, and the virile lines of his face became harsh; his mouth thinned. Wentworth had seen defeat close on his heels in a hundred battles with the geniuses of evil, but never before had he sunk to this low stage, stripped of fortune and home, of all resources. His two trusty companions, Ram Singh and Jackson, who had fought with him through so many years of travail, were in prison, charged with assisting the Spider to escape from the police, and now it seemed he was hunted by some new rising criminal power—perhaps the same which had caused the death of that girl so terribly. Since it was not the police, who else would dare to trail the Spider?

Nita stirred restlessly beneath his ministrations. "You've reached the end of your rope, dear," she said slowly. "Don't you think it's time to... to think of ourselves a little?"

Wentworth continued to stroke her forehead, wordless. Rarely did Nita van Sloan weaken from the pledge of mutual service they had made. No woman was more brave... His throat swelled....

"Kirkpatrick sent a message?" he asked shortly.

16

"Yes," Nita sighed. "Stanley says it's time to rest on your laurels. He says he wants your pledge that you will never again become the Spider or do the Spider's work. He intends to create an under-cover bureau which will work as you have in the past, and there is no need for you to risk your life—and mine—any longer. It's what he says, Dick, not I."

"Go on," Wentworth told her, drily.

Nita thrust up on her arms, looked earnestly into Wentworth's face. "Dick, haven't you done enough? Haven't we suffered, sacrificed enough? Surely, we've earned..." Her voice broke, her head hung forward a little, and Wentworth put an arm about her shoulders. Her voice was muffled when she went on. "Dick, I don't often speak like this. But years are passing, lover. We are... not getting younger. There's gray in your hair, above your temples...."

WENTWORTH LAUGHED suddenly, harshly. He heaved himself to his feet, strode across the room and back again, stood stiffly beside the bed. "It's hard enough, Nita," he said, "Don't, please, make it any more so...."

Her braced arms supported her body, and the head with its tousled chestnut curls was thrown back. "But I want to make it hard. I want to make it so hard that you'll..." Her eyes were half-closed, her lips parted. "Dick," she said, "Dick, lover, don't you love me any more?"

Wentworth dropped to his knees, buried his head against her. Nita's hand brushed back the crisp, black hair from his forehead, gently.

"We can't," Wentworth said between his teeth. "Nita, dear, we've fought this over so many times. How could we be happy knowing that we stole our happiness from others? It's not vanity, but there is no other man who can do the things I do, who can stop these fiends who forever rise to prey upon humanity. If we took our happiness at the cost of others… Even tonight I saw a girl killed—terribly—and it looks as if some new madman has arisen…."

"Kirkpatrick says," Nita still spoke softly, "that unless you promise him that the Spider will stay dead, he will see to it that your estate remains confiscated. He will throw the entire power of the police force—all his men—upon the task of finding and capturing you. He doesn't want to do it, but he will. He says, you must give him your promise."

Wentworth drew slowly to his feet, stood staring before him. His mouth twisted.

"You wouldn't be foolish enough, Dick, to let mere pride drive you?" Nita cried. "You're not vain enough to hold out, just because Kirkpatrick tries to force your hand?"

Wentworth shook his head. "No, it isn't vanity. If I believed it was for the best, I would do what Kirkpatrick wants. But I cannot. If I did… Do you think that the police can combat the new menace even now arising? Do you think that anyone with the forces of the law can strike terror as does the Spider?"

Nita got slowly to her feet. "Then you won't promise, Dick? Not even for my sake? Not even to keep Kirkpatrick from breaking his heart over you? He loves you, Dick. He is doing this for your own good...."

Wentworth smiled with a bitter twist of his lips. "I believe that," he said slowly, "but the answer can be only one thing, Nita."

Nita stood before him, her eyes filled with pleading. "For my sake...."

Wentworth's whole body was rigid. He looked at Nita, and there was no longer a smile on his lips.

"Dearest," he whispered, "I cannot. *I cannot!*"

Nita's arms sagged hopelessly. "All right, Dick," she said. "Then this is the end."

A violent crash on the door put an exclamation point to her sentence. The flimsy portal swung wide and a man stepped into the room with a revolver in each hand.

"It's the law, Wentworth," he announced calmly. "You're under arrest!"

CHAPTER 3
THE HORROR AT
HEADQUARTERS

WENTWORTH STARED at the detective and words formed themselves in his brain. "Nita has betrayed me!"

He realized that he staggered backward a step, not with surprise or fear at the man's entrance, but at the mad thought that had struck his brain and heart. *Nita has betrayed me!* It wasn't possible, and yet how else had the police found him here? His stricken face swung toward Nita....

She stood with her hands twisted together, her brimming eyes on his. "I did it," she whispered low. "Yes, I brought him here. Oh, Dick, you must realize that you have no chance. Won't you promise Kirkpatrick what he asks?"

Wentworth laughed harshly, thrust out his wrists for the handcuffs which the detective was fumbling from his belt. He laughed again, then sank his teeth into his lip....

"Please, Dick," Nita came closer to him, whispering. "Please, Dick, understand that... you *must* promise."

Wentworth slowly forced the madness from his brain. He looked again at Nita. She winced, but her eyes did not falter. "Please, Dick...!"

Wentworth felt the cold shock of the steel shackles closing on his wrists. He started uncontrollably, but did not take his eyes from Nita's. "I'm trying... to understand," he said heavily.

The detective looked from one to the other of them, hesitated to hurry Wentworth from the room. It was very clear that Wentworth's arrest for murder meant little to him beside the fact that it was this woman who had brought about the capture. The detective thought of his own wife. How would he feel if Tony sold him out…?

"Hell!" said the detective roughly. "Come on out of this, Wentworth."

With a physical effort, Wentworth pulled his eyes away from Nita and glanced at the detective. His face was familiar in some way….

"I know you're tricky," the policeman said, "but don't think you can get away." He grinned abruptly. "You taught me once, Spider, how important good shooting is. I learned the lesson well. Don't make me shoot you."

Wentworth shook his head slowly. He said, "No."

It had been easy, terribly easy, for Nita to betray him. She had simply arranged for the detective to follow her, but not to act until she had had a chance to explain Kirkpatrick's demands. Her *"This is the end…"* had been a signal. Wentworth shrugged, started for the door.

The detective stepped in front of him. "Wait a minute, Spider," he said, "Listen, I'm Bill Horace. You remember me, don't you? When you were fighting the guy that called himself the Death Fiddler, you saved my life once, and you gave me a break that got me a promotion to detective. You remember? Now, listen, Spider, I like you a hell of a lot. Don't make me shoot you, will you?"

Wentworth looked him directly in the eyes. Yes, he remembered the man well enough now. A clean, hard-fighting cop. He said dully: "Until I reach Kirkpatrick's office and your responsibility ends, I promise you I won't attempt to escape."

Detective Bill Horace grinned widely, shoved his gun into its holster. "Gee, that's fine, Spider. Thanks a lot. Come on, let's go."

WENTWORTH'S LIPS twisted bitterly. Yes, everyone trusted the Spider. Let him once give his word, and not even the police doubted he would keep it. Trusted by everyone, yet his sweetheart had betrayed him....

"All right," he agreed flatly. "Will you carry my suitcase?" He thought absently that the luggage contained the habiliments of the Spider. If it were opened... Somehow it did not seem to matter now.

Nita's hand rested on his arm as they moved toward the door. "Please, Dick," she whispered. "I did it for your sake. You know that. Can't you see the police are bound to win in the end—bound to capture or kill you? Dick, for your own sake—for mine—won't you promise Kirkpatrick what he asks?"

Wentworth looked at her, and his smile became suddenly gentle. "I don't hold it against you, dear. I know you think this is for the best—that what Kirkpatrick asks is reasonable and necessary. But you didn't see that girl die tonight. You can't know... as to the police, I could escape from Horace any time I wanted."

Horace said: "Hey! What is this?" He threw a quick glance about the hotel lobby, which they had reached, strode to his prisoner and set the suitcase down.

Wentworth smiled at him. "I gave you my word I won't escape before your authority is ended. That should satisfy you."

A gay-colored feathered dart was fixed in Cassidy's cheek!

Horace bent over the handcuffs to inspect them.

Wentworth said: "It would be very easy to hit you under the chin with the bracelets, Horace."

Horace jerked back, his gun coming out. Then he shook his head ruefully. "I guess I was made a dick too soon," he acknowledged wryly.

He took them to the sedan he had parked in front of the hotel and they went swiftly through the dark, cold streets toward headquarters. Nita was crying softly beside Wentworth, one hand upon his arm. He could not quite comprehend the situation. Aside from her hope that he would yield, Nita would have to stand trial for the deeds of the Spider. Why, once she had snatched him from the death cell itself on the very night when he was to have been executed!... Uncertainty shook him. She *had* betrayed him to the police. He looked curiously at her bent head. He had known women to do strange things to the men they loved....

The sedan drew to a halt in front of headquarters and Horace kept a gun on Wentworth while they walked up the steps and into the building, upstairs again to the square, barren office of Commissioner Kirkpatrick. It was three o'clock in the morning, but Kirkpatrick was there. He rose austerely behind his desk

"I was afraid he wouldn't promise," he said shortly, his words clipped, incisive as always. "For God's sake, Dick, use some sense."

Wentworth shrugged, sat down on a chair against the wall, jauntily crossing his legs. "Could I have a cigarette, Kirk?" he asked quietly.

Kirkpatrick strode toward him, the long, decisive stride that Wentworth knew so well, leaned over to light the cigarette. Kirkpatrick's saturnine face was set harshly. Deep lines were etched about his mouth corners and though his military mustache was inky  black, there was a stippling of silver at his temples. Wentworth thought of what Nita had said about the gray in his own hair and he smiled, sucking in a lung-full of smoke.

"We're getting old, Kirk," he said conversationally. "You expect from me a pledge you should know you can't extract—and I allow a woman to betray me."

Nita gasped, "Oh, no, Dick!"

Kirkpatrick straightened, frowning at him. "No, I didn't expect it, but Nita begged me to let her try. Listen, Dick, why not be reasonable about these battles with the Underworld? If you must fight, let me make you a deputy commissioner of police. You can help me. God knows I'll be glad to have your help. You've been invaluable to me in more than one case...."

Wentworth lifted his mocking brows. "Thank you, Kirk."

"Go to hell," rasped Kirkpatrick. "Why aren't you content to do these things legally, instead of stealing around like a thief in the night, murdering men, putting that nasty little red seal upon their foreheads? I can't understand it, Dick. How can a man of your fine sensibilities be a merciless killer like the Spider?"

Wentworth lifted his cuffed hands to his lips, removed the

cigarette and exhaled slowly. "I see that you're riding your hobby-horse again. Still convinced, Kirk, that I'm the Spider?"

KIRKPATRICK SNORTED and flung himself into his seat. "Why not be reasonable, Dick?" he said again. "Accept the appointment as my deputy!"

"Aren't you forgetting a number of warrants charging me with murder?" Wentworth said casually.

Kirkpatrick cut the air with the side of his hand. "Stop evading me, Dick. Won't you accept this appointment and stop this damnable… Spidering? The Spider is dead, Dick. Let him stay dead. You can fight just as well…."

"Wait a minute, Kirk," said Wentworth. He snapped the cigarette to the floor, set his foot upon it. "I know the Spider pretty well. Let me give you his answer, as I know he would give it. The Spider is no more marvelous, no more extraordinary than anyone of your detectives—say than Bill Horace here. Granting of course that your detective is well educated, as Bill is; that he has practiced with his guns until he can use them like parts of his own body and that he knows a few other rudiments of defense and offense.

"Your men are hamstrung by a lot of legal foolishness. They can't shoot at a criminal unless he has a gun in his hand and tries to use it, unless he makes a grab for a gun; or unless the officer's life is in danger. Things like that. He must gather evidence which will hold water in court against the pyrotechniques of a lawyer which the crook's money will buy, sometimes against bribery and framed alibis. You know yourself a dozen men who should be hanged, yet they walk the streets beyond your reach. Why?

Because your men must follow legal procedure. The Spider, if he were convinced of the guilt of anyone of those men, could exact the laws penalty with none of the laws delays and uncertainties."

Wentworth was leaning far forward, his eyes holding Commissioner Kirkpatrick's. He was very earnest. This was his apologia. This was why he had become the Spider—why he had turned his back upon the felicities of normal life and thrown his very soul into the struggle against injustice and crime. Wentworth jerked to his feet, hammered on:

"When you can guarantee that courts and juries cannot be bribed, when you can slice through the legal red-tape which protects the guilty, when you can arm your men with the right to enforce the law fearlessly and without respect to favoritism, there will be rest for the Spider. Why, today, a new menace has arisen to harass the people of your city. That girl who died tonight. You don't know about her yet, but I…!"

Wentworth whirled toward the window with a cry. The glass was tinkling to the floor and a rock bounded across the office.

"Down, down for your lives!" Wentworth shouted. A fearful premonition of disaster raced coldly over him. "Get out of range of the window!"

Kirkpatrick threw himself to one side of the broken window, snatching out his gun. Detective Bill Horace started forward, and Wentworth tripped him to the floor. Nita already had thrown herself prone, and Wentworth hurled his weight bodily atop Horace to hold him down.

Even as Wentworth acted, the door whipped open and

Cassidy, the red-headed watchdog of Kirkpatrick's office, came plunging in, gun in hand.

"Down!" Wentworth shouted at him.

But it was already too late. Blended with his voice was the metallic pop of an air gun fired in the street and something flashed through the air in a glittering arc ending in Cassidy's face. Either he did not see the missile, or had no time to dodge. It struck him, and he reeled back, his hand jerking up. A gay-feathered dart quivered in his cheek!

"Pull it out, Cassidy!" Wentworth cried. "Pull it out, before…!"

He wriggled off Horace's body, crawled toward Cassidy, his mind sick with horror. The ceiling light went out with the crash of a shot within the room and Wentworth whipped his head about, made out Kirkpatrick's broad shoulders against the gray oblong of the window. The Commissioner had shot out the light. His long-barreled revolver roared once, twice. Alarm bells were ringing throughout the building and the shouts of men added to the din. Through it came the quiet voice of Kirkpatrick, speaking into the telephone on his desk

"There is no further danger. Send men out to pick up the dead man in the street. I shot him. Also send the electrician to my office."

WENTWORTH WAS already on his feet, lunging toward Cassidy. No need to shout at him again. The paralyzing effect of the drug must already have numbed his brain. Perhaps if someone pulled out that dart… Cassidy was still motionless just inside the door, for a moment longer, as Wentworth moved toward him, he stood there rigidly, his stiffened body outlined against the light from the outer office. Then a jerking, convulsive shiver ran over him, his feet made quick, jumping thrusts at the floor. He began to run in tight, crazy circles....

Wentworth lifted his handcuffed hands to knock Cassidy out, then checked himself. If he were seen doing it... "Knock him out, Horace," Wentworth ordered harshly, "Knock him out!"

Cassidy ceased his running, whirled on his toes like a dervish, jumping up and down as he spun. From his throat, there issued a hoarse, wordless cry that went on and on and on....

"For God's sake, knock him out!" Wentworth shouted.

Kirkpatrick strode from behind his desk, echoed the order and Horace jerked from his paralysis of horror and strode forward. Cassidy continued his mad gyrations, his screaming terrible in the darkness, until Horace struck swiftly with a blackjack. Cassidy crumpled to the floor. He lay in the oblong of light that slanted through the open door from the outer office and his arms and legs still jerked and his breath was stentorian. Kirkpatrick flicked on a flashlight which glared whitely on the unconscious man's face, brought out the toy dart in vivid contrast.

"In God's name," Kirkpatrick rasped, "what is it? What made him do that?"

"That," said Wentworth furiously, "is the weapon of the newest menace to rise against the people of the city. Within an hour, Cassidy will die, as that girl I mentioned died this evening. Nothing on earth can prevent it, and whatever period of time between now and his death that he is conscious, he will dance and scream."

Nita's shuddering moan fell upon a tense silence, broken only by the harsh breathing of the stricken Cassidy. Then Wentworth's voice rang like a challenging trumpet.

"Kirkpatrick, this is the newest thing your men must face. Do you still demand that the Spider remain dead?"

CHAPTER 4
MURDER GONE MAD!

K IRKPATRICK HAD gone down on his knees beside the twitching body of Cassidy, had plucked out the feathered dart. At Wentworth's challenge, he looked up at him, grave-eyed, somber. Already his face was drawn with the horror he knew must lie ahead.

"Yes, Dick," he said quietly. "I need you, shall always need you terribly. Please, don't make me fight you."

Wentworth met his gaze, frowning. A police officer thrust through the doorway and Kirkpatrick told him to get Cassidy into an ambulance, rush him to the hospital. Cassidy was carried away and once more Kirkpatrick faced his friend. Wentworth felt his appeal deeply. He knew that Kirkpatrick had accepted the nomination for governor three years ago largely to keep from having to fight his friend, the Spider, whose work for humanity he respected and admired. Nita pleading, and now Kirkpatrick....

"Please, Dick," Kirkpatrick was repeating, his clipped accent deep with emotion. "I've warned you before and I do it again. Give me your word or there will be an end of the Spider. It has been years since the police have thrown their whole strength into a hunt for him. Refuse, and I warn you... Hell, Dick, you know I don't want to do this! Give me your promise and help me!"

Wentworth smiled, looked from Kirkpatrick to Nita and saw that Detective Bill Horace was at his elbow, grinning hopefully. Damn it, these people loved him, and he had to refuse them. As always, he was the only one who thought whole-heartedly of the service of others. These others thought of him and of themselves.

"Sorry, Kirk," Wentworth said quietly, "the answer is no."

He brought up his handcuffs and caught Kirkpatrick beneath the chin, swung the shackles sideways with the same motion and struck Horace, just starting into action, on the forehead. He had to hit Horace a second time before the detective slumped to the floor. Wentworth bent calmly over him and found the handcuff key. Nita caught his arm.

"Oh, Dick, please, please!" she whispered. "Don't you understand what this means? Kirkpatrick will throw every man he has on your trail. You won't stand a chance...."

Wentworth freed his hands, straightened to look at Nita. He smiled at her, in the sudden boyish way he had, caught her close into his arms.

"Yes, darling, I understand," he said. He kissed her warmly. "And I understand why you tricked me into a capture. But it won't do. I can't... There's no use going into all that again. Good-bye, sweetheart."

Nita clung to him, but he put her hands away, stooped to recover his guns from Horace. He got them and heard Nita, half across the room, say sharply:

Nita Van Sloan

"Put your hands up, Dick!"

He straightened slowly, holstering his guns and looked at her. She had Kirkpatrick's long-barreled revolver leveled at him. She knew how to use guns, too. Wentworth had taught her himself.

"I'm not going to let you," Nita sobbed. "I won't allow you to destroy yourself this way. For God's sake, Dick, don't make me...."

Wentworth moved slowly toward her, his eyes holding hers. "You wouldn't...!" he began, and saw abruptly that she would. The gun was aimed steadily at his left thigh. He drew in a deep breath. "All right, Nita," he said. "You can surrender me to the police, but I'll only escape later, and some one may get hurt in the process. It would be much better if you let me go now." Wentworth's jaw was locked hard so that he had to force the words out and there was a swelling coldness in his breast. Nita, *Nita* was doing this to him! He knew her motives, but she was betraying him, destroying….

NITA WAVERED on her feet, her face dead white. "Oh, Dick," she whispered. "You won't change, and you're hating me. I can see it in your eyes." She laughed with abrupt harshness that was strange in her soft voice. "It was bound to end this way. Bound to. Lover…."

Wentworth took a quick step forward, halted at the renewed menace of the gun. Kirkpatrick was stirring on the floor. Within seconds, he would recover consciousness and Wentworth's chance to escape would be gone… "Very well, Nita," he said quietly, "you'll have to shoot me." He moved, slowly, deliberately toward the gun. Nita looked at him with her violet eyes widening, her lip caught between her teeth. Wentworth's own

teeth were set hard together. God above, what was he—what was Nita—doing to their love? But it wasn't that, really. It was their love which was doing this thing to them. He took another step forward… Nita screamed. It was a faint, hoarse little cry, scarcely audible even to Wentworth. She jerked up the gun and pressed it to her own temple, pulled the trigger.…

Her movement was swift, but so was Wentworth's. He was the Spider and his life had depended more times than he could remember on the ability to move like lightning. He knew what to do, too. No attempt to grab the wrist. That would have been too slow. His fist struck her clenched hand, jolted the muzzle upward as she pulled the trigger. The bullet blasted her close little hat from her head, and Nita dropped to the floor. Wentworth smashed down on his knees, caught up her limp body in his arms.

"Darling, darling!" he cried. "Please…!"

The scent of scorched hair was in his nostrils. Madness of grief beat at his brain. Then he laughed brokenly. She was not hurt, had only fainted… For another swift moment, Wentworth held the woman he loved close in his arms. He bent, kissed her lips, thought that hers answered, as if, even in the depths of senselessness, his kiss could reach her soul. With a muffled sob, he sprang to his feet. He could not delay. Already that shot had set the alarm bells to ringing. He dropped his suitcase out the window, bounded to the doorway, to the hall, crouched in the doorway of a darkened office while three policemen pounded past, then darted to the steps. He moved swiftly then, but without furtiveness. An officer sprang into the hall. Wentworth pointed a hand up the steps.

"Quick!" he shouted, "They tried to kill the Commissioner. I'm going out and take them from outside...."

The cop bounded up the steps and Wentworth reached the sidewalk, got his suitcase. Bill Horace's car was still parked there, but the key was not in the switch. Wentworth walked off along the street....

He fought to force his mind to the issues which confronted him, to the business of locating the killer behind the use of the feathered dart that brought horror and death, but the memory of Nita's misery and her pleas rose to devil him. He sought out a cheap hotel, flung himself down to sleep. Usually, he could force his brain to almost instantaneous rest; but tonight, relief refused to come until he had tossed for hours. More than once, Wentworth laughed bitterly at his own misery. This was the ultimate folly of the Spider, severing himself from the last ties which remained to him upon earth so that he might continue his thankless battles. He had only one consolation, the knowledge that unless he persisted, this new and rising terror might gain complete ascendancy over the people he loved and served....

IF HE had been bitter the night before, the morning and a glimpse of the newspaper headlines filled his cup to overflowing. He read there the story of his betrayal by Nita, of his capture and transportation to police headquarters. That was bad enough, but *Kirkpatrick had blamed him for the death of Cassidy!* The feathered red dart which had brought the Dancing Death to the policeman was called "a new and fiendish device of the Spider." The body of the girl Wentworth had tried to save had been found also, the cause of her death discovered and *that also was blamed upon the Spider!* The newspaper sobbed over the girl, one Elsie Blackmon, and cried down vengeance on the head of the Spider. She was a bride, it seemed, and she had been hurrying home from her office to prepare supper for her husband, a mechanic, when she had been seized.

Wentworth read these things while he ate his breakfast in a small restaurant, and anger began to tremble through his body. Whatever else he might expect of Kirkpatrick, this deliberate lying was not among them. Kirkpatrick was assiduous on his duty, almost to the point of fanaticism, but he never before had compromised his honor. He had threatened to throw all his power against the Spider, and he had done so terribly!

According to the newspaper, Wentworth had knocked Nita van Sloan cold with a blow of his pistol. The marvel was, the story ran on, that he had not killed the woman who had betrayed him—that he had not affixed his red seal to her forehead. The Spider's whole history was recorded, the fact that twice he had been believed dead and each time had returned to kill and kill again... The newspaper fell from Wentworth's hands and he strode from the restaurant with his meal scarcely touched. For hours, he strode the crowded streets of the city in such a turmoil of mind and spirit as he had rarely known, careless of the possibility of recognition by the scores of policemen whom he passed.

It was mid-afternoon when he realized with a start that he was within a few blocks of Nita's home in the Riverside Towers. For a moment he stood, wavering, but he shook his head slowly.

There was no need to torture himself—and Nita—any further. He glanced about over the traffic of upper Broadway, moved heavily toward a subway entrance. Resolutely, he fought off the feeling of depression which had settled upon him. The Spider should be used to injustice by now. It was not the first time he had been falsely accused. It was only that his dearest love and his most intimate friend....

Wentworth's head jerked up with a start and instinctively, he hurled himself to the pavement beside the platform entrance to the subway kiosk. He had heard the staccato voice of machine guns too often not to recognize their death laughter... Beside him, a newsboy uttered a gasp and his body was hammered against the side of his stand, pinned there by successive bullets, and finally allowed to crumple bloodily to the pavement. An old woman, caught in the hurricane of lead, was hurled down the subway steps, her thin scream dying almost before it was born. Only Wentworth's prompt action had saved him. His guns leaped to his hands. For the moment, he thought that some enemy had spotted him and cut loose with the gun in utter disregard of the safety of others in the crowd. But instantly he saw his mistake. A battered old car was careening down Broadway and from the back seat a man with his face twisted into a screaming mask was strewing deadly bullets widespread along the crowded sidewalks. There were two men on the front seat, one driving, the other using a pistol....

WENTWORTH'S GUNS went into swift action. He snapped one shot before the milling crowd closed in between him and the car, but that one bullet was deadly. It struck the machine gunner in the face, smashed him backward out of sight. For a moment, the hammer of the death weapon was silent, then it began to stutter again. With an oath, Wentworth sprang to his feet, looking about for some means of pursuit. A taxi stood at the curb, its windshield in a thousand shining shards, the driver slumped to the floor. From beneath the door, blood seeped in rusty drops....

With a single leap, Wentworth reached the running board, yanked open the door. The sight of the driver made his gorge rise, but he thrust the dead man aside, kicked the starter and lurched in pursuit of the murder car. It was three blocks ahead and the machine gun still stuttered and coughed out death. The sidewalks were strewn with dead and dying people. The screams of the wounded were shrill and hoarse. And then Wentworth saw a horror beside which all this other paled into insignificance. Among the stricken men and women, others screamed and *danced!* They whirled and spun to the death beat of the guns as if it were the music of fearful drums. Into each, one of the poisoned darts, had been plunged. A girl of fifteen jumped up and down in a corybantic frenzy beside a baby carriage which dripped with the red wine of murder.

Savagely, Wentworth sent the car leaping forward. A sedan, its driver dead, had half-climbed the island park dividing the two driveways of Broadway. There was not room enough between that and a stalled truck for the taxi to pass. Wentworth slammed into the sedan at full speed, wedged its front aside and went caroming on in pursuit of the murder car. All along the path of pursuit, dozens of people died and others whirled to the furious music of the poisoned darts. Wentworth's lips moved with silent curses. He strained forward in the seat as if with his straining body he would lend the taxi speed.

Eight blocks from the kiosk where be had been standing—eight blocks of carnage—Wentworth came within seventy-five feet of the battered old car. He eased a gun from its holster and, choosing his time well, fired twice in quick succession. The left rear tire of the car ahead exploded under the prick of the bullets and the auto yawed wildly toward the central island. Glass smashed from the rear window and the muzzle of a machine gun began to spurt death toward the Spider.

Wentworth lifted his sure gun and the death chatter ceased. The car was still veering madly. Wentworth coaxed the taxi to more speed, surged to the right so that he could see the driver. His lips twisted as he pulled the trigger once more... and the slaughter was ended. The car wrenched completely about, skidded, hit a traffic standard and overturned, landing flat on its top, crumpled like a tin can. The tires spun idly.

Brakes pulled the taxi up in a shrieking halt beside the wreck and Wentworth leaped to the ground. Beneath the overturned car, nothing stirred. He circled and saw that one of the men had attempted to leap free at the last moment. He had been caught beneath the edge, pinned flat on his back. He was very dead. Wentworth laughed sharply. He whipped a platinum cigarette-lighter from his pocket and bent over the dead man. Then he sprang into the taxi and raced away....

When the police found the man who had done this thing, they might have a counter-argument to present the newspapers about the Spider. For there on the forehead of the men who had slaughtered the innocents, Wentworth had left his seal, the glittering red symbol of his vengeance, with the hairy legs and venomous fangs of the Spider! A half-dozen blocks away, Wentworth flung from the taxi and darted down a subway entrance. Down there, the trains ran as before with a great, hollow rumbling and it seemed strange that they should do so when up above the streets ran red....

ONCE MORE, Wentworth threw back his head and laughed, harshly, terribly. A man looked at him uneasily, rose and left the car. Oh, he was mad, right enough—mad with the desire to strike at the men who could do such things as had been done up there on the streets. For a while, the Spider had faltered beneath a load of personal grief, but he would not hesitate again. He knew abruptly what he must do and how he would do it. Those men who had watched him must come from those who were behind the slaughter. It was sure that they did not come from the police, for otherwise there would have been no need for Nita to betray him. Who else than those who planned such fearful carnage would fear and stalk the Spider? Well, he would return and make sure the watchers found him! If murder was their purpose, so much the better. The Spider would wreak added vengeance for the dead!

It took Wentworth forty minutes to reach the East Side slum street where he had lived during the weeks of his hiding. He looked about him, without appearing to search, but he found no trace of the watchers. He never had, though. Perhaps they were there... Quickly, he unlocked the door, sped upward along the dim stairway, entered his room. From the chair beside the window, a young man arose slowly, stiffly. His shoulders were bowed, his eyes rimmed with red. On the window-sill were the remains of a half-hundred cigarettes....

"What are you doing in here?" Wentworth demanded sharply.

"This is your room?" said the man.

Wentworth nodded. "Yes, and I want to know...."

The man reached into the chair and got a revolver. His face twisted slowly, terribly. He took a heavy step toward Wentworth.

"You killed my wife," he muttered thickly. "Now, I kill... *you!*"

He leveled the revolver, fired point-blank at Wentworth.

CHAPTER 5
CHOICE OF DEATH

WENTWORTH HAD ample warning of what was going to happen, time enough to shoot the man behind the gun at least three times—but the very words spoken made it inconceivable that he should fire. It was apparent that this was no hired gunman... Wentworth made no effort to draw. He sagged against the wall as if driven by the bullet, but actually he had moved before the flash. He slumped to the floor, rolled to his back. If the man wanted a second shot, Wentworth would have to fire on him—but if he was content....

The man walked heavily forward and stood over Wentworth with the gun sagging from his fingers. He let it drop and fell to his knees. His face lifted.

"Elsie, Elsie!" he whispered.

Wentworth opened his eyes widely and studied the lifted face, saw the grease-rimmed nails of the man's hands and memory glinted like a sword. Elsie was the name of the girl who had been killed by the feathered dart—Elsie Blackmon. Her husband was a mechanic and the Spider had been blamed for her death! This then was her husband, intent on vengeance. But how had he learned that the Spider lurked here? There was only one explanation. The enemies of the Spider, those who had trailed him so long, had led the man here.

Without a sound, Wentworth's hand went to the revolver the man had dropped. He rolled sharply, came to his feet with the gun pointed.

"Just stay on your knees for a moment, Blackmon," Wentworth ordered quietly.

Through long seconds, the man stared with incredulous eyes. Then he lurched to his feet, started forward with his fingers crooked in menace, stopped only when the revolver muzzle dug hard into his belly.

"I didn't kill your Elsie," Wentworth informed him sharply. "I didn't—kill—her. I shot the man who did. Do you hear, Blackmon? I shot the man that did it in his right arm. But I didn't kill Elsie."

Blackmon swayed back from the gun muzzle. He had a frank, honest face, a high, sloping forehead contorted now by scowling uncertainty. He was stupefied with grief, robbed of his bride, racked by the desire for vengeance… He wanted to charge into that gun muzzle, but he was nevertheless afraid of it.

"Who told you I did it?" Wentworth insisted.

Blackmon moved his wide shoulders. "They did, and then the newspapers...."

"Whom do you mean by 'they?'"

Blackmon hesitated. He lifted a hand, dragged it across his forehead. His shoulder muscles flinched, and the hand moved hesitantly toward the back of his neck, then swung limply to his side. He swayed slightly. A sharp and fearful suspicion seized Wentworth. He sprang abruptly, to the left, out of range of the open window, and peered at Blackmon. What he saw confirmed his shrewd guess. In the back of Blackmon's neck, there flowered a bright feathered dart!

With a curse, Wentworth dived at Blackmon's legs, spilled the man to the floor. It was the work of an instant to whip the dart from the flesh. He snatched a knife from his pocket, slashed the flesh, put his lips to the wound.

Wentworth could never afterwards tell why he wanted so desperately to save the life of this bereaved man. Certainly he no longer needed him for contact with his enemies. They were there, outside the window somewhere, possibly ready to shoot another dart. It would be simple for the Spider to trail them, yet he applied himself to the task of saving Blackmon.

CLEARLY, WENTWORTH saw the plot of those who

spread the Dancing Death to rid themselves of the Spider through the agency of a man they had bereaved... He worked swiftly, drawing poison from the wound he had deepened, spitting it upon the floor. He stopped only when the rasp of a footstep at the doorway pulled up his head. His hand flew to his gun, but he was already looking into the muzzle of an automatic, held steadily by a smiling man.

"Cease your labors of love, my friend," the man directed softly. "Arise, and come with me."

Wentworth stared at the debonair gunman. He seemed slight, yet was as tall as Wentworth. His smile shone whitely beneath a dapper mustache and the hand which aimed the gun was long-fingered, carefully tended.

"Must I again bid you arise?" the man asked gently.

Wentworth saw death in the shine of those large black eyes. He got deliberately to his feet, made no attempt to reach his revolvers. He read ruthless efficiency in the long-fingered hand holding the gun. The man's entire person was as carefully tended as that hand. His dress was almost foppish, yet too well selected and cleverly tailored to be conspicuous.

Wentworth's voice deepened with irony. "And whom have I the honor of addressing?"

The man uncovered his head, bowed faultlessly—and did not let the gun waver. "Señor Arana—" he said mockingly—"Mr. Spider, I am Señor Pascual Madrigas y Hialenda. Will you be so kind as to accompany me?"

Wentworth moved forward willingly. There was no doubt in his mind that this man who styled himself so grandiloquently

was one of those behind the Dancing Death, probably one of the leaders. Since the man had not killed him
outright, it was obvious he intended to
take him to some headquarters of the
criminals.

That was precisely what the Spider
wanted. It would have been better,
of course, not to go as a prisoner, but
even that did not concern him greatly.
Before this, the Spider had gone as a prisoner into the camp of
the enemy—and the enemy had bitterly regretted it!

Wentworth stepped into the darkness of the hallway and
something silk-soft snapped about his throat from behind.
Instantly, it became a band of steel and a hard knee ground
into his spine… It was useless to struggle. If he reached for a
gun, those wrenching thumbs could snap his neck vertebrae in
a breath….

"No, no, Raj!" came the soft voice of Señor Madrigas, "I do
not want him killed… just yet—"

Wentworth had just time enough to realize that he had been
seized by one of those stranglers of the East known as *Thugs.*
Then dark, beating waves of pain engulfed his consciousness
and he knew no more….

THERE WAS no aching wrench about Wentworth's recovery; no throbbing head, nor rasping throat. He drifted back, and
that puzzled him, especially the absence of pain in his throat.
He slitted his eyes and peered upward between the lashes.

Above him, there was an azure ceiling dappled with golden stars, patently artificial, but exquisitely executed. Wentworth's sense of bewilderment increased. If he had been murdered while unconscious, it would be much easier to understand than this. His fingers, moving cautiously at his side, closed on soft silk....

With a mental shrug, Wentworth opened his eyes wide, sat erect and looked about him. He was alone in a room whose walls were draped in soft, blue silks. The divan on which he had lain was a pile of multi-hued pillows. He looked at his unbound arms and legs and a slow smile touched his lips. He was garbed in the long, loose robes of the East and there were felt slippers on his feet. A jeweled knife-hilt protruded from a sash about his waist, probably a sham haft without a blade. What was the purpose of all this mummery? He had no way of telling, but he might as well play the part for which he had been cast....

He drew his hands together, letting the loose sleeves of his gown fall back along lean, browned forearms. Then he struck his palms together softly, three times. If everything else was in accordance to his environment, a *genie*—or at the very least, a Nubian slave—should part the drapes, and....

The curtains directly across the room were drawn aside to reveal an emaciated Hindu who swept a low *salaam*. "What does my master desire?" he asked harshly.

Wentworth caught the gleam of the black eyes, studied the muscular hands. "Leave my presence, dog!" he said in scathing Hindustani. "Pig and son of a pig, thou Thug. Away, before I destroy thee."

The Hindu flinched before the torrent of abuse, cringed

against the wall. His eyes glittered with hatred, but failed to meet the assault of Wentworth's glare.

"A thousand pardons!" he muttered. "Thy servant was sent...."

"Out of my presence!" Wentworth thundered and finally the Hindu slunk away. Wentworth allowed his face to show no symptom of satisfaction. He leaned back upon his cushions, toyed with the hilt of the knife. His tirade had shown him at least one thing. For the present, he was not to be treated entirely as a prisoner. There was an unfavorable aspect, of course. The masters of the Dancing Death must be very sure of him, their headquarters must be extremely well guarded....

It was useless as yet to attempt any plans, so Wentworth did what few men could have accomplished in his position. He forced all speculation and worry from his mind, relaxed and simply waited. He could not strike until he knew more of his environment....

It was fifteen minutes before the curtains swayed again and a soft footstep sounded within the room. Wentworth did not glance that way. Keeping his eyes upon the floor before him, he toyed moodily with the knife. He continued to delay for five full minutes and during that time there was no sound at all. Finally, he lifted his gaze, and had to fight to maintain the impassivity of his face. A woman stood just inside the curtains—a woman out of the Arabian Nights. She was slim—even small—and the shadow of her limbs through her diaphanous garments was graceful. Her girdle was fine brocade, like her scanty jacket, and at ankle and wrist, there were bangles of gold....

THESE THINGS Wentworth saw in a swift glance. Her

eyes, which saluted him above a brief veil, were long and of a liquid green like fire. The woman *salaamed* and, with slow gestures, unfastened the pearl-sewn cord which supported her veil. Wentworth's eyes narrowed. By that act, the baring of the face, an Eastern woman would designate herself as his slave! It was ridiculous, all this. In God's name, what had happened since that strangler's cord had bitten into his throat? He reminded himself—and it was bewilderingly necessary to do so—that not

SENOR MADRIGAS

THE DOCTOR

"THE CHIEF"

TARSA

long ago, he had faced Blackmon, a man intent on his murder—
that he had been captured by wanton killers in the midst of
one of the gravest crises the Spider had ever faced. Was it the
purpose of his captors to bemuse him?

Wentworth scanned the revealed face of the woman, the long,
pale line of the mouth, the intelligence of her brilliant eyes. He
nodded graciously.

"Come," he said gently, "and tell me many things."

The woman's eyes were veiled for a moment by their lids and
Wentworth would have sworn that a ghost of a smile touched
the pale lips. She came meekly forward and sank upon her knees.

"What is it that my master wishes to know?"

Wentworth delayed answering while he studied her face
closely. Her black hair was a cloud across her shoulders, drawn
from her temples by a pearl-set fillet of gold. The brows were
straight and black, the forehead intelligent, but there was a hint
of… of cruelty about the curved nostrils.

Without warning, Wentworth shot out his hand, set his
fingers about the slender column of her throat, shut off her
breathing. Her green eyes flew wide with terror, her mouth
opened in a soundless cry. She struggled, snatched at the knife
in Wentworth's sash, but he held her powerless while her face
slowly darkened with strangulation.

Her eyes rolled up, and Wentworth released her, let her fall
limply to the floor at his knees. Then he sat impassively, watching her gasp air into her lungs. His lips twitched once painfully.
It was not to his liking—this thing he had done—but he had
known at a glance that this woman was no mere odalisque sent

to serve him nor yet the woman of one of the leaders. There was too much keen intelligence in her face. She was a leader herself, and....

Slowly, the woman pushed her body up from the floor.

"A warning, my dear," Wentworth whispered, mockingly, "A matter of teaching you what you may expect should I suspect you of treachery." He put a hand on her shoulder and she winced, but obeyed the pressure and leaned closer. She was still panting and her head came up heavily, as if the weight of her hair dragged it down. She lifted her face until her eyes met his. There was bewilderment in her gaze, and dawning hatred. Slowly, Wentworth bent toward her, wound his fingers into her hair. The woman's eyes widened, then were veiled by her lids; her mouth parted....

WENTWORTH DID not like the methods he used, but he understood women as he knew men, and he had realized instantly how he must tame this green-eyed hellion. Personal choice had nothing to do with it. He must discover the plans—the strengths and weaknesses—of these torture killers and thwart them. If he could pierce this woman's armor....

He thought he had. Watching him under heavy lids, the woman lifted her hands slowly to arrange her hair. She moved languorously, with the heaviness of sensory repletion. The East was in every posture of her alluring grace and when she spoke, there was an indefinable slurring of words, at once elusive and enchanting. Her skin was golden....

She laughed at him suddenly. "Are you always so precipitate, Señor Spider?"

Wentworth smiled slightly, made no other answer.

51

"Are you still curious," she asked him presently, "about… many things?" She was trying to regain her original poise, but the warmth of her eyes betrayed her. Finally, she rose slowly to her feet and clapped her palms softly together. A very modern and western French maid entered with lowered eyes and put a woolen cloak about the woman's shoulders. For a tenth of a second, as she turned to leave again, her gaze met Wentworth's. He smothered a curse and the Eastern woman laughed.

"I'm sure," she murmured, "that your technique finds admirers." She held out a hand, "Come! Since you won't ask questions, I must show you what I think you'll like to see." She drew his arm about her waist. "Call me Tarsa," Her green eyes glanced up at him.

"Put on your veil," Wentworth ordered shortly.

Submissively, but with a mockery that was unmistakable, the woman who called herself Tarsa obeyed him. She drew the cloak close about her, held back the draperies while Wentworth stalked through the doorway. He still was far from understanding what was happening, but he was beginning to have an idea. The Spider had a name to conjure with in criminal circles. The killers would realize that the keen strategy with which he had often defeated the Underworld might be used just as well to overcome the forces of the Law….

The hallway was spacious and Wentworth moved slowly in the direction Tarsa indicated. He did not obviously look about him, but his eyes took in all his surroundings. He saw that the windows along one side of the hallway were barred. Tarsa stopped finally before a doorway which was painted a brilliant

scarlet and touched its middle panel with the tips of her slender fingers. For a space of seconds, nothing happened. Then a previously invisible peephole opened and an instant later, the door slid sideways into the wall. A young Japanese, white-cloaked and trousered, beamed at them through thick-lensed glasses.

The man hissed politely, bowed three times and stepped aside. Wentworth strode through ahead of Tarsa and his swift glance revealed a singularly complete and elaborate laboratory. At the sound of their footsteps, a man jerked about from a bench where an involved creation of tubes and retorts was steaming over a row of Bunsen burners. He came toward Tarsa with quick, shuffling steps, smiling widely. He ducked in three quick bows as the Japanese had, glanced toward Wentworth, all the while smiling.

"Ach, what iss it we haf here?" he rumbled. His fingers were stubby and fat, stained with chemicals. His blue eyes were very kindly and he puffed incessantly at a malodorous, black cigar.

"Doctor," Tarsa's voice was crisp and authoritative, "I want you to show the newest member of our league the results of your latest experiment."

THE DOCTOR ducked his head in swift bows again, swung toward his bench and touched a switch. The laboratory immediately went dark and it was apparent that the far wall was of ground glass, for upon its screen—or perhaps behind it—shadow figures began to move. They became clearer, were visible now as rats creeping about in a large pen. There were fully a dozen of the huge, gray beasts.

"You will haf to take my vord that they are healthy specimens," said the doctor cheerfully. "Now, vatch. I this button touch so, and…."

A cloud of some dark vapor spurted down from the top of the pen. The rats darted away, then turned to face it with bared teeth. For the moment, that was all. And then, one of the rats… *screamed!* It was not a squeak in the ordinary sense in which rodents make noise, but a cry of anguish almost human in its terror and pain. More of them were shrieking now. They dashed about in frantic circles, bit at each other and at their own bodies, climbed the walls of the pen, struggled and spun. That phase lasted only for seconds; then their hind legs began to give way under them, collapsed in paralysis, while the rest of their bodies retained their full vigor and strength. Then, before Wentworth's eyes, the rats *began to disappear!*

Wentworth watched with a slow fury rising within him. No need to ask what was the purpose of this fearful experiment. In this enormously efficient laboratory, the criminals behind the Dancing Death sought new murder weapons! His gaze was riveted in a fearful fascination upon the rats. They were not disappearing in the metaphysical sense of the word, but their bodies, beginning at the rearmost portion, were… were melting, *dissolving away into nothingness!*

"You haf seen snails *hein?*" whispered the Doctor, "Haf perhabs sprinkled salt on them when you were *ein Knabe,* a boy, *hein?* You haf seen snails melt away as the salt touches them? So! Ve haf found the salt that melts avay animal bodies!"

An uncontrollable shudder jerked at Wentworth's muscles. It was incredible, the thing that he had seen, but the rats' bodies had almost disappeared now, apparently with ghastly torture, for as long as the rats retained enough substance, they continued to scream in mortal agony... Wentworth lifted a hand that was suddenly trembling to his forehead, palmed the moisture there. If those fiends ever loosed that terror upon humanity...!

Wentworth felt Tarsa's hand touch his arm like a caress.

"My master," she whispered. "We know what this will do to human bodies, but we have not yet had a prisoner on whom to test the Dissolver. The darts... We tried to persuade a young woman to volunteer for that—perhaps you remember Elsie Blackmon?—but you interfered and the experiment had to be enacted there on the street. It was most... successful."

Wentworth uttered grim laughter. The rats were silent at last. The final fragments of their bodies were dissolving....

"I hope," whispered Tarsa, "that we have to... search... for a volunteer, my master."

Wentworth's hands clamped into hard fists at his sides as Tarsa led the way back across the laboratory. He needed no translation of Tarsa's final remark. If the Spider did not fall in with their plans, they would not have to search for a "volunteer." They would test the Dissolver—on Wentworth!

CHAPTER 6
COLD STEEL RECEPTION

A T THE door of the laboratory, Wentworth dawdled, looking about again while the Japanese manipulated the door. The Doctor already was bent over his complicated set-up of chemical tubes. Rage was swelling in Wentworth's throat, but he held himself rigidly in check. The Doctor was not the leader. He was a fiend, and he must be destroyed, but first the Spider must find the directing genius. Until that time, he would have to dissemble, mislead the woman, Tarsa.

He stalked firmly into the hallway. "Are there more wonders to show me?" he asked mockingly. It was typical of the Spider that in his dilemma, even with the vision of the death before him, he did not think of himself, but of the benefit to his people. It was not escape, but vengeance, that he planned.

Tarsa laughed lightly, her hand approvingly upon his arm. "Many wonders," she told him. "Let me go first here."

She walked lithely ahead of him, cloak drawn close about the modeling of her hips, and stood directly before a pot which contained some grotesque and strange plant. She lifted her right arm straight above her head and Wentworth counted his pulse beats to time the interval. Forty-one heart beats… Tarsa turned and beckoned.

"Infra-red lights and a photo-electric cell," she informed him. "If I had failed to release the trigger of the trap, you and I both would have been perforated by a dozen darts. In fact, by this time, we should have been dancing to the death music that only the dying can hear."

Wentworth said drily, "I appreciate your courtesy. You are right, though. There are still things I want to know. I would like to meet your leader. He must be a truly formidable person to have organized and contrived such things."

Tarsa smiled at him strangely. "Yes," she said, "but that must come later. Aren't you curious as to how our men trailed you, and how we set Blackmon on your trail?"

"Not especially," Wentworth answered with a shrug. Tarsa moved to the wall and a doorway he had not previously seen opened to admit her. He strode with swift caution after her, found himself back in the room he had quitted.

"Such indifference must be rewarded," Tarsa told him. "Have you forgotten your little escapades under the *nom de guerre* of Corporal Death?"

Wentworth dropped onto the divan, smiled but did not answer. So that was how it had been done! During his last battle with the Underworld—at that time under the leadership of Senator Hoey—it had been necessary that the Spider seem to be dead, so he had fought under a new title, Corporal Death. He had had certain comrades and it was evident that the forces of Tarsa's allies had traced him from them....

"We could not be sure of your identity," Tarsa said pleasantly, "and unless Corporal Death took a hand in the affair, we didn't see any point in antagonizing him. Once we were sure that he was the Spider..." She was on the cushions before him, and leaned abruptly forward, put her hand upon his knee. "Spider, we need you badly. Admitted that we have potent weapons, we still have no one who can plan and direct as you can. I'll make no petty bargain with you. Throw in with us and you can have

Sweeping the great sword upward,

Wentworth leaped to the kill!

whatever you want—without any limitation at all." Her smile
was languorous with meaning. "Nor will I threaten....

"Spider, has the city and your friends used you well? Look

how Kirkpatrick framed you for that murder in his office, even that woman…" Tarsa's voice broke off with a gasp as Wentworth lifted his blue-gray eyes coldly to hers. "Very well, I'll skip that part of it. But you were betrayed. Are you going to be a sap all your life?"

WENTWORTH HAD dropped his gaze after that single involuntary flash when Tarsa had spoken slightingly of Nita van Sloan. What the woman said did not stir him, but the old bitterness—which had risen at first knowledge of the treacherous weapon Kirkpatrick employed against him—did come back. Nothing this woman could offer or say would even rival the plea that Nita had made….

He smiled into Tarsa's face and her green eyes blazed with hope. "Throw in with us, Spider?"

"I want to meet the chief before I commit myself one way or the other," Wentworth told her. "I certainly won't serve under a man I've never seen."

"Not under, Spider!" Tarsa cried gaily, "Side by side! But I must have your promise first, your promise to throw in with us."

Wentworth shook his head and for a long moment his blue-gray eyes held hers. His gaze was very steady, very determined. "I won't say a word until I've seen him."

"None of us has seen him, Spider. Please promise!" Tarsa was urgent, almost beseeching. "He never shows himself except in a long, black robe, with a hood over his face. I… I…" She rose gracefully to her feet, gathered her woolen cloak over her arm and stood looking at Wentworth. Her voice became abruptly harsh. "I risk my life to take him your demand. I hope you appreciate it, Spider."

"Does a man appreciate service from his slave?" Wentworth was stern, though he said it with a smile.

Tarsa stooped swiftly, sought his lips. Then she ran from the room. Wentworth was instantly on his feet, across the chamber before the curtains had fairly swung back into place. If Tarsa was too absorbed with the Spider's charm to see the trap he planned, it was not likely her chief would be. He would simply refuse to see Wentworth and demand a decision on pain of death. Of course, the Spider had no intention of yielding. He only wanted to see the Chief so that he could kill him....

Wentworth whipped aside the curtains and spied along the hall. Tarsa's rosy heels flickered out of sight around a corner twenty feet away and Wentworth ran, soft-footed in felt slippers, after her. The way led again past the strange potted plant and, this time, Tarsa *salaamed* before it and, bringing her hands close to the floor, she flickered them back and forth, from side to side, in a queer, broken rhythm. Wentworth, watching moved his own hands in swift imitation. It was too intricate to remember with the eye alone. He must have the additional prompting of his muscular reflexes....

Tarsa straightened, whirled and a door opened in the wall two paces further along. She ran to it, stepped through and the door closed.

Wentworth moved rapidly toward the plant. Had Tarsa first held her arm into the air to prevent the trap from being sprung, or did the other movements take care of protection from the hidden darts also? If both actions were unnecessary, it might well be that manipulating both would either sound an alarm or riddle him with the arrows of the Dancing Death! Wentworth's lips set grimly as he neared the plant. He had only seconds to decide. His mere presence in the hall here was a declaration of warfare that could only end—if he were caught—in his "volunteering" to test the Dissolver!

He stopped before the grotesque plant, faced it and *salaamed*, began to flicker his two hands back and forth the way Tarsa had done. He had made his decision on the basis of probability. It was unlikely that the method of opening the door safely would be one that would require so long a lapse of time as first holding an arm into the air for half a minute and then executing the *salaam*. He finished the movement, pivoted toward the door and his lips curved in an abrupt, quiet smile. The door was opening! SCARCELY WAITING until it was entirely open, Wentworth leaped forward and through the aperture. He heard the well-oiled machinery begin to operate again, closing the door, and found himself in a narrow, long room, draped as his own had been in silken curtains. He had no opportunity to observe it, even to guess at the direction in which Tarsa had gone. The arras parted ahead of him and a giant Negro, his hugely muscled torso bare above the waist, stepped into his path with a great, curved, two-handed sword clenched to strike.

"Tarsa!" Wentworth shot at him. "I come for Tarsa!"

The Negro hesitated. It was all that Wentworth could hope for. The bluff would not carry him far, and he must leave no killers to block his retreat after he had killed the Chief. And God knew this great two-handed sword would be an obstacle. He recognized the type at once, knew its beautiful balance and the havoc it could wreak, when properly used. It was of the type used by Japanese warriors in ancient days and was known as a *tsurugi*. It was not overlong, perhaps forty inches, but within its circle, nothing could live… Yet Wentworth walked steadily forward beneath the poised terror of that sword. When he was within the distance of a single stride, he whipped his hand to the knife hilt at his belt and leaped. He expected the hilt to prove a dummy—without a blade—but the Negro would scarcely know that. It would serve to bluff him….

The knife hilt came clear with a shrill whisper of steel and Wentworth found an efficient blade in his hand. He laughed softly, and punched with the short knife as the Negro tried to whip the two-handed scimitar down upon him. Wentworth's thrust sped with all the force and power of a fencing master and the steel slid between the Negro's ribs, pierced his heart and sent him reeling backward against the curtains he had parted, dying….

Wentworth snatched the big sword from relaxing hands, prepared to ease the Negro's body to the floor when it recoiled from the wall. But it did not recoil. The curtains belled backward under the pressure of the dead giant's fall, whipped upward and Wentworth had a brief view of a large, crimson-draped chamber—of a figure in black hood and robe twisting to face the commotion. Then the curtains whipped down again and hid all that.

With a shout he could not repress, Wentworth sprang past

the body of the Negro, lunged through the curtains with the huge, keen *tsurugi* ready to strike—and checked, staring. The room, in which, a moment before, the hooded leader of the killers had stood, was empty. There was not even a rustle of a curtain to show where the man had vanished. Behind him, Wentworth caught a whisper of sound. He started to whirl, but it was already too late. Silk brushed his throat, became a band of steel as a knee gouged into his spine. He was wrenched backward with a violence that stabbed him with nausea…. But this time, Wentworth held a formidable weapon in his hands. He twisted the *tsurugi,* and cut viciously downward and backward as if to split his own body in two. Even as he struck, he saw two Hindus, stripped to loin cloths and turbans, rip through the curtains ahead, racing to seize his wrists, to hold him a helpless victim for the Thug who had struck from behind.

It was an awkward blow that Wentworth struck, but the weight of the weapon made up for that. The man on his back shrieked, gurgled. The impetus of the weapon drove Wentworth forward and he felt warm liquid spurt across his shoulders and knew that it was his would-be murderer's blood. The strangling silk had gone lax… The two Hindus coming toward him across the room raced on to the attack They snatched out their heavy, curved knives, sharpened on the inner edge and made for ripping upward into a man's body….

WENTWORTH DID not attempt to check his forward lunge, which was the result of the sword driving his victim's body against his shoulders. He altered its direction, sent himself to the left side of the man who was on his own left. Thus he not only forced the Hindu to pivot in order to use his knife, but temporarily blocked the man's companion. As he leaped, he twisted the sword once more, brought its incarnadined edge sweeping toward the turbaned head.

It was a close thing at best. Wentworth had known that when his swift brain determined on the only action he could take. A knife, lifting upward from the hip, can strike in less than half the time of a two-handed, over-head slash. Wentworth's shoulders, his whole body went into the speeding of that blow. His blue-gray gaze bored into the fanaticism of the Hindu's black look. The Thug had pivoted like a flash, starting his stab at the same moment, but he had not quite calculated the distance. He was forced to take a sharp stride forward, hoping to come inside the sweep of the sword… Wentworth crooked his elbows, leaned back against the impetus of the swing and arched the sword through.

The curved weapon of the East must be used in a dragging motion at the moment of contact to achieve the maximum damage with its keen edge. So operated, the *tsurugi* could slash more terribly than any beam-like weapon of the old Crusaders which could, when fiercely swung, cut a horse in half. Wentworth's sword struck the head of the Hindu near the hilt while the weapon was still only a few degrees forward of vertical. As he completed the stroke, leaning back, pulling through, the edge ate through bone as if it were moist clay.

The face of the second Hindu, leaping to the attack, was terribly distorted, with his lips shrinking back from dirty yellow, rotted teeth, the disemboweling knife held ready. Wentworth sprang backward, twisting and wrenching at the same moment to free his blade. The sword completed its downward slash, and pulled free. The Hindu fell to the floor, and Wentworth whirled toward his new enemy. There was no time to lift the blade for a downward stroke. Wentworth sprang forward, whipping the twice-wetted sword upward in a diagonal slash. It was a time for swift, unerring action. An instant's hesitation would mean certain death—and out of the corner of his eye, Wentworth saw the curtains to his right sway, whip aside!

His immediate assailant had checked his charge beyond the end of the flickering blade, and now, as the great *tsurugi* swept upward, pulling Wentworth's body violently out of line with the momentum of its swing, the Hindu leaped forward to the kill! At the same moment, the rising curtain revealed the browned legs of four other Hindus with ready knives—and Tarsa, gripping a heavy automatic pistol in her right hand! Even as he glimpsed her, caught the deadly narrowing of her long, green eyes, she lifted the gun and leveled it, within point-blank range, directly at his breast!

CHAPTER 7
THE SPIDER SPRINGS A TRAP

WENTWORTH HAD known the direful possibilities for him—had known that if he missed the stroke he would be pulled off balance and rendered easy prey for a swift knife thrust. The Hindu's assault was dangerous enough, God knew, but to confront a heavy gun also, at the same time… If he had read death in the eyes of the Hindu he had killed, what he saw in those of Tarsa must be torture lust! It was her narrowing green glare which decided Wentworth on action in that split-second when the pull of the sword exposed his left side to the inleaping Hindu and Tarsa leveled her gun.

Wentworth released his hold on the sword, sent it flashing, circling, straight at Tarsa's gun! Simultaneously, he checked his body, faltered backward. He was still off-balance, but the Hindu had already started his thrust. He turned the blade, tried to reach out—and the thick, thirsty knife snatched at Wentworth's silken robe, grazed the flesh of his abdomen....

A shot blasted out and steel vibrated into sound, a shivering, silvery note. Then Tarsa screamed. Wentworth could not look to see what had happened there—could not glance yet toward the four knifemen who had ranged themselves beside the woman. The blade was perilously close. It would take only a twist of the wrist, a raking drag to gash his body from side to side... Wentworth's left hand closed on the knife-wrist and he changed his backward stagger into a powerful leap.

The maneuver caught the Hindu in mid-spring, still surging forward to the attack, and the sudden yank at right-angles to his course was like snapping the tip of a whip. He was not thrown to the floor, but his onslaught was broken and he reeled drunkenly across the room.

Wentworth could glance then toward the others who ringed him in. Tarsa was scrambling on the floor. A Hindu bent over to assist her to her feet. She was wringing her gun-wrist and it was apparent that the great *tsurugi* had not struck her with the cutting edge. Suddenly Wentworth laughed aloud. He snatched up the knife the dead Hindu had dropped and lunged toward the four men and Tarsa.

They must have thought he had gone abruptly mad—or that he had some hidden and terrible weapon—for they faltered, flinched from his charge. It was all that Wentworth needed. Within ten feet of the cringing Hindus, he swooped to the floor and snatched up Tarsa's automatic from where the sword had knocked it. Even as it plopped solidly into his palm, his finger groped for the trigger. The shot went wild, of course, but it held the men back for another instant and Wentworth danced backward, dragging the heavy two-handed sword with one hand, gripping the automatic with the other. Even with his superbly coördinated power, he could not swing the *tsurugi* one-handed effectively, but these others, staring at the red which dribbled down its gray steel, would be thinking not of that but of how horribly it had killed….

Wentworth saw a knife arm flash back for a throw and billeted a bullet in the man's brain. He fired twice more and pinned two frantic Hindus to the wall with his heavy lead. A forty-five caliber bullet strikes with the force of more than six hundred foot-pounds, like the fury of three hefty football demons all concentrated in an area less than one inch across. When those men were struck, they went down and stayed down. The fourth Hindu fled with a thin, nasal scream pouring from his lips and Wentworth fired through the curtains after him. The scream stopped. Tarsa stood where she had risen to her feet. She no longer massaged her wrist, but faced Wentworth with her chin high, her green eyes narrow and fearless. Wentworth weighed the automatic on his palm.

"There should be one shot left in this," he said, eyeing her. "Take me to the Chief."

THROUGH DISTANT corridors, he could hear wild alarum shouts. Nearer at hand, a man yelped like a dog on a trail. Tarsa smiled slowly into Wentworth's eyes.

"There is another bullet, my master," she mocked him, "but I will not take you to the Chief!"

Wentworth knew determination when he saw it. He nodded slowly, drew the hilt of the *tsurugi* up through his sash, then moved toward Tarsa. He put his hand lightly on her throat as he had when he strangled her:

"Very well," he said quietly, "you will not take me to the Chief. But you will go with me, and you will be quiet."

She smiled at him above the lean strength of his hand. "Yes, my master!"

Behind him, across the width of the room and along the hall by which he had entered this chamber, the alarums were growing louder. Wentworth gestured to Tarsa to turn about and he thrust her along the way she and her four men had come. His bullet had caught the Hindu who had fled through the neck It had smashed his spine and face… Wentworth's face grew white and grim.

"So you add dum-dum bullets to your other accomplishments, Tarsa?" he breathed.

Tarsa shrugged, a smile on her lips. "If you had not been so very lucky with your sword, my master, you would have discovered how effective they are. My bullet hit the blade."

Wentworth smiled, too. "People persist in calling my skill luck. Could luck last forever?"

Tarsa laughed aloud. It was a harsh and hateful sound. *"Yours won't!"*

Wentworth glanced at her curiously as they moved through a series of dim rooms scantily furnished with low divans and eighteen-inch tables. She had fired on him with a dum-dum bullet and now threatened him with death, yet if he were to take her by the throat, or in his arms… She shied away from him, glancing almost with fright into his face. Her green eyes were pleading. Abruptly, she stopped beside a dim-glowing light, pulled on its chain. The light went out and Wentworth reached swiftly, caught her wrists. She did not try to escape, but pulled the light chain again—darkness, light, darkness, light—in slow sequence, then swiftly: darkness, and light. A trap door slid open in the floor almost at their feet and the four top steps of a steep flight were illuminated. Tarsa gestured, her eyes veiled.

"After you, my master."

Wentworth shook his head in slow negation and Tarsa shrugged, sat down on the edge of the trap and groped for the steps. Abruptly, she ducked and the door slid back, into its sockets so swiftly that even Wentworth's swift reflexes could not block it. As the panel flicked shut, Wentworth caught a transitory glimpse of her face, her long, pale lips curved in a mocking smile. Furiously, he reached for the chain of the light, began yanking it in the rhythm she had shown him. He finished the slow sequence, tensed his fingers for the final two pulls and hesitated. Caution goaded him. He tore a strip from the edge of his robe, tied it to the chain and stepped back three full paces to make the two final pulls.

The thing that happened was lightning-like in its rapidity. Two blades shot from one wall, pivoting like a whirled scimitar. Three slashed out of the other wall and the knives interlocked, speeding in opposite directions. It was just a glimmer of light, then the keen steel had vanished. Wentworth stood, still holding the strip of silk which had released this diabolical trap; and felt a warm flush wash over his body. If the caution that must ever walk beside him had not prompted him, his body would lie now in segments on the floor. Those sword blades had spanned the hallway from wall to wall!

AN EVEN graver peril hung over him and it made Wentworth whirl and speed back the way he had come through the dimly lit chambers. Tarsa was free. She knew where he was and the courses he must follow in flight. It would take her only seconds to set the Hindus all his trail… and there was only one bullet in the automatic. Wentworth freed the sword, held it in his right hand, clasped his gun in the left. They expected him to make a break for freedom, it would only prove that they did not know the Spider. His work would not be done until he had slain the Chief—and not until his work was finished would the Spider think of personal safety….

He passed through the chamber where the dead lay. A pity he did not have the Spider seal with which he marked criminal dead! It would be fitting rival for the symbol of Kali, the

Destroyer, which the Thugs wore upon their foreheads. Well, there was a way. The first Spider seal had been wrought in blood upon the forehead of a criminal. The Spider's finger would make an excellent brush, and thanks to the *tsurugi*, there was pigment enough....

Disguise was impossible for the Spider without some materials, but at least he could alter his appearance somewhat. He stripped baggy trousers of red silk from the Nubian guard, donned a turban from a dead Hindu's head. His silken robe was stained with blood and he dabbed his chest with it. Then, naked to the waist, sword ready in both hands, he hurried out into the hallway where the strange plant sat in its pot and where there were windows barred with steel.

The corridor was deserted but Wentworth walked warily, his eyes lancing ahead. This emptiness might be inspired by fear, but it was much more likely a trap... He reached the entrance to the room where he had first recovered consciousness and ducked inside. Here, of all places, they would be least apt to search for him. He lay on his side behind the low divan, arranged pillows and wall curtains to conceal him—and waited. He had no definite plan of action, simply that he would seize on any opportunity to find and kill the Chief.

Men had called the Spider many harsh names—butcher and murderer, killer of the night. Some, who could not imagine altruism or any unselfish motive had even accused him of hi-jacking wealth from the criminals he apparently fought. If any of those could have seen him now, waiting with only a single shot in his gun to battle against incredible odds—and this only to put an end to the mad slaughter of the innocents—they would have to admit that, whatever else he might be, he was not a coward.

For two hours, Wentworth lay there patiently, waiting for his chance to strike. He saw nothing, heard nothing save swift, furtive footsteps occasionally passing in the hall. Finally, his muscles tensed to the swish of the curtains at the entrance. The draperies were thrown high and a Hindu, clothed in white tunic and trousers instead of the loin cloth of the others bowed low. Tarsa walked meditatively into the room. She crossed directly toward the divan, settled herself slowly upon it while the Hindu stood with shoulders braced far back, facing her as if awaiting orders. A glimpse of the man's face startled Wentworth. He wore the full beard of a Sikh, as Wentworth's own body servant, Ram Singh, who was in prison for helping him, was accustomed to do.

Tarsa spoke in Hindustani, which Wentworth understood perfectly: "Convey to Madrigas *sahib* my congratulations on his capture of the Spider. Tell him to kill him immediately next time. You will captain the party on the pier while Madrigas *sahib* commands aboard the *Picardie*. When you have cleaned up the pier, you and your men will follow the *Picardie* down the bay and help repulse any attack *Jao! Go!*"

THE SIKH swept a low *salaam*, lifting his cupped hands to his forehead. *"Han, memsahib,"* he murmured, deep-voiced, and backed from the room. Behind the divan, Wentworth held his breath, waiting. What he had already heard caused him a shock of horror. The *Picardie* was the largest passenger ship afloat. In days when other vessels went begging, she would carry her full quota of wealth and prominence. Here indeed would be rich looting for men who could wield such a panic-stirring weapon as the Dancing Death or—Good God!—suppose they used the Dissolver! Wentworth had to take a tight hold upon himself, to keep his tensing muscles quiet. His hands ached to close about the throat of this woman who could participate in such infamy.

Another Hindu bowed his way through the curtains and Tarsa rose smoothly to her feet, stepped toward him. "Yes, the Dissolver is to go, too," she said quietly. In the hallway outside, Wentworth heard her strike her hands sharply together, heard a rush of swift, soft feet. His lips thinned. There was no doubt in his mind that he had been discovered. How could Tarsa have helped hearing even his muted breathing? They had been so close together that he could have touched her without extending his arm. He should have strangled her when he had had the chance....

Wentworth did not lie—as another man might have done—waiting for the attack, hoping against certainty that he had not been discovered. He rose deftly to his feet, skirted the left wall of the room until he stood just inside the doorway. The pistol was in his sash, the heavy sword in his hands. It was not according to his desire, the battle that he must fight now. If he could learn no more about the plans to attack the *Picardie* he wanted to escape from this den of killers and warn the police.

So Wentworth stilled the cry within him that urged a headlong attack on the men who were gathering outside. He slipped under the silken drapes which hung clear of the walls and made

74

himself inconspicuous beside the doorway. He could not hope to steal away without being detected, but at least....

His thoughts chopped off as a Hindu stepped through the curtains scarcely a yard from where he stood and stalked, stately, into the room. He crossed the floor and stood on one side of the divan, arms folded, his back toward the spot where, apparently, Wentworth was suspected of hiding. Hardly had he taken his position when another man advanced and took a corresponding place on the other side of the divan. They were the first of six who ranged themselves so. Wentworth's interest mounted swiftly. Either this was a clever plan to overwhelm him or these men were preparing for the entrance of the Chief himself. No lesser person would have such an escort....

SCARCELY HAD the thought crossed his mind when two Hindus whipped back the curtains and stood at rigid attention. Through the opening they made stalked a figure cased in black robes. Grim triumph tightened Wentworth's jaw as the robed figure seated himself upon the divan. The two men at the door dropped the draperies into place and stood with arms folded. They were inside the curtains, Wentworth was outside, peering through a break in the silk. It would have been the work of an instant to slip out into the hallway and flee. He would have done that but for one thing—that black-robed figure upon the divan. This was the man who was behind the hundred atrocious murders that had been contrived. This was the man who had ordered the looting of the *Picardie*....

It was important that Wentworth escape to issue the warning, but it was even more important to eliminate this mad butcher. There could be no second thought about that. Despite these overwhelming odds, the Spider must strike this blow for humanity. He would probably be killed in the next thirty seconds but he did not even think of that. He gripped the sword in his right hand, drew the automatic which contained one bullet. He could have shot the Chief from behind the draperies, but the Spider did not wipe out even such vermin as these without giving them their chance....

Wentworth took a long pace to his left until he stood behind the two door-guards. With two swift blows, struck through the silken draperies, he hurled them unconscious to the floor, then he sprang full into the chamber, a terrifying figure with his naked torso daubed with blood, the stained sword ready in his right hand. He leveled the automatic at the black-robed figure on the divan.

"The compliments of the Spider!" Wentworth cried and sent his flat, mocking laughter over the room. He aimed the automatic at the forehead of the black-robed Chief and pulled the trigger and—*the gun did not discharge!*

The figure in black laughed exultantly and, with a curse, Wentworth realized that he had taken Tarsa's word, and his own count, that there was one bullet left in the gun. It was ridiculous, but he *had* counted on an empty pistol to destroy the greatest menace that had ever risen to terrify humanity! The thought was a lightning flash. The Hindus were snatching knives from their sashes, leaning forward to the charge. The way was still open to the door....

Sharply, behind him, rang out Tarsa's cool voice. "Do not let him escape alive!" she shouted clearly and through the doorway he had believed open rushed another trio of the knife-armed Hindus! Wentworth spun toward them, hurled his empty automatic into their faces and with both powerful arms whipped up the mighty *tsurugi*. The Spider threw back his head and laughed.... This was the end...!

CHAPTER 8
RENDEZVOUS WITH DEATH!

BEFORE THE threat of that uplifted decapitator— and the courage of a man who laughed at death—the charge of those men faltered for a moment as Wentworth had hoped it might. When they wavered, he whirled, leaped with down-swinging sword straight for the black-hooded figure on the divan! It was daringly conceived and perfectly executed, that attack. Nothing could save the Chief, though he struggled to his feet and threw both arms protectingly above his head.

The fierce sword whispered dreadfully as it swept down. No mortal flesh and bone could stay its greedy arc. Wentworth exhibited his amazing dexterity with a heavy blade, struck a mighty, lethal blow. The Chief tottered, slumped forward at the Spider's feet. He whirled to face his enemies, and once more he laughed. It was mocking, that laughter. It was a challenge and a taunt, the slogan of a battle-drunk man. So the Spider faced his doom....

As before, the men hung back, on one side of the room. If Wentworth had worn the ancient silk-and-iron armor which went with the *tsurugi*, they could not hope to prevail against him, but he had not even a shirt to his back. His naked chest pumped to his laughter.

"Come and meet the blood drinker!" he taunted them in Hindustani, shaking the heavy sword. "My sword is still thirsty. Come, let me spill thy red blood upon this floor; let me decorate these blue silken walls with crimson…" He swung the blade gently before him, his muscles cording through his chest and arms, and the steel whispered with a harsh, dry hissing as if indeed it were thirsty.…

Behind the ranks of his assailants, stood Tarsa. Her automatic was in hand. She could have ended this battle with a single shot, but she held her fire. There was a green fire in her eyes, her lips were parted from locked teeth. She panted.

"In, dogs!" she cried at the Hindus. "In, dogs, and slay him! Tear him to pieces. Kali feasts this day!"

The men surged forward together, ripping knives poised, but only a couple could reach Wentworth as he stood just clear of the wall, only a few could actually close at once. They tried to rush him, to choke the swing of that mighty sword, and Wentworth leaped backward and whipped the razor tip across two throats. The third man ducked low, coming in with an arm curved above his head, his knife hand reaching out. Wentworth deflected his downward cut, caught him just back of the left ear, cutting under the left jawbone and forward… There were three bodies in the ring before him now, and a slippery floor to make footing difficult for his assailants. The returning side-stroke of the sword caught the wrist of a fourth man and fist and knife struck the wall. The Hindu screamed and fought his panic way back through the ranks, gripping the stump. There was a muffled cough of a gun and Tarsa lifted the smoking automatic above her head.

"In, dogs!" she cried. "He who flees... *dies!*"

The dogs held back. Three men lay terribly dead upon the floor and a fourth had died at the hands of their mistress, and still the sword was thirsty. One of the remaining Hindus whipped back his arm and flung a knife, but it was not made for throwing. Its curved blade made it travel awkwardly and the *tsurugi* struck it in mid-air, battered it to the floor.

"Charge!" Tarsa hurled at them. "Altogether."

The men hung back, muttering. "Nay, shoot him, *memsahib*. Why should thy servants give the sword to drink when thou hast a gun?"

"In, dogs!" Tarsa thrust through the ranks herself, stood in the forefront, but clear of the sword's reach. Her eyes met Wentworth's and she laughed, as he had laughed, drunk with the battle she had witnessed. "Surrender, fool," she cried at him. "You haven't a chance to survive." But her eyes bade him fight on....

THE SPIDER balanced the sword before him, a guard against her automatic. It was mad of her not to use it, but her primitive passions were stirred. Men died in agony around her and she laughed. If he triumphed over these others, there would still be her gun to face. Strength pumped hotly through Wentworth's veins. He sprang forward sharply, flailing with the sword, striking right and left, whirling the whispering blade in glittering circles about his head. Tarsa sprang backward lightly, her

gun held ready and Wentworth could not reach her. Men fell
again before that thirsty edge.

The rest pressed upon him, slashing out with their knives,
ducking and leaping back. One of them whipped the body of
a comrade from the barricade of death and hurled it at Wentworth. If it had struck even his legs the Spider must have fallen.
He leaped aside, met the body with a slash of the sword that
hammered it back, but he had been forced to retreat a full yard
and he could no longer swing the sword about his head in great,
flailing circles lest it strike the wall and jar it from his hand. The
men had closed in that yard and crouched, just out of reach of
the sword, waiting their chance.

From Wentworth's left a man leapt in. There was no time to
strike with the heavy *tsurugi*. Wentworth stabbed with the knife,
gashed the wrist, but the thrust came on with the weight of the
Hindu behind it, bit into his thigh. Wentworth struck again and
the man fell dying from a throat wound. The *tsurugi* circled, and
men who had sprung closer cringed back

Wentworth's strength was drained. If he had only a light
swift rapier....

Wentworth let the remaining men drive him back to the
wall, hedge him in with darting knives. He dropped to one knee.
Triumph gleamed in the faces of the Hindus. Within moments,
they would avenge their slain comrades. Already his powerful
right arm could scarcely wield the blade....

With a curse, Wentworth hurled his knife into the face of a
Hindu who encroached too close and the man screamed with
rage and fear, his nose broken. With both hands again on the

sword, the Spider struck about him violently for a few moments and the Hindus shrank back to wait until the flurry was finished. Wentworth let the blade touch the floor, idle before him and they looked into each other's eyes, appraising enemies before the end… And the Hindus began to edge closer again.

Wentworth let the sole remaining Hindu reach a point on his left from which he could stab, waited until the knife ripped toward his throat. Then he caught the man's wrist, twisted the knife free while he yanked the Hindu toward him, flat on his face. The knife struck down and the Hindu quivered.

Wentworth let the dead man sag. There was but one enemy left to fight him—a woman with a gun!

WENTWORTH GLANCED at her, saw that she was smiling sardonically. She held the automatic aimed straight at him. Was this the end? Had he gone through all this carnage only to fall now? With catlike swiftness, he hurled the heavy blade at the woman, not intending to strike her. But when she flinched from the arc of the hurtling blade, Wentworth, who had leaped the moment the *tsurugi* left his hand, lunged across the room and catapulted himself against her.

His body bore her backward to the floor, and she lay there, motionless, without a sound. He snatched up her automatic, stood staring down at her. Her head was pillowed on a fallen servitor, and the concussion of the blow had stunned her. Her dainty, brocaded jacket was gummed with blood; her diaphanous garments clung to her limbs.

A sudden thought struck Wentworth. He hunted around, found the body of the slain Chief. He fumbled off the black-slitted hood and frowned in bewilderment. The man he had killed, the one he had taken for the Chief was no more than a Hindu like the rest, with the mark of Kali, the Destroyer, on his forehead. Great God! He had been tricked, lured into a supposedly fatal trap while the servitors of the Chief sped about their slaughter and the looting of the *Picardie!*

So Tarsa was one of the fiends behind the murders of the Dancing Death—a leader of some sort, for these Hindus obeyed her. Rage tore at Wentworth's heart. He found a knife, poised it over her breast. She should die… The Spider had never killed a woman. Women leaders had been killed, yes, but never by his hand. Surely she had paid a large penalty here in the slaughter of her men. Hers could be no great part in the operations of the Chief. Slowly, Wentworth lifted the knife again. He dipped his finger in blood and upon Tarsa's left breast he inscribed the dread, scarlet symbol of the Spider. It was his warning. It she persisted….

Upon the forehead of the man whom Wentworth had believed the Chief he once more inscribed the seal of the Spider. Then he strode rapidly from the room. It came over him overwhelmingly that he had no idea at all of the place in which he had been held prisoner. He might be hours away from New York and the pier from which the *Picardie* would sail. He remembered that between his capture and his recovery of consciousness, there had been time for his throat to recover from the soreness of the strangler's cord… Furthermore, the cold winds of January whined outside and Wentworth was naked to the waist.

He hunted swiftly for clothing and was finally compelled to

don the garments of some of the men he had slain. It neces-
sitated maintaining his partial disguise, but that might prove
helpful. He went once more to the barred windows of the corridor and, peering out of them, detected some hint of a street
ahead. He worked his way toward that through the twisted
hallways, moving with light caution, his eyes searching ahead
of him. He had seen a few of the fiendish traps which helped to
guard this place and did not wish to fall into such a death now
that he was speeding to warn and protect the *Picardie.*

He found a door finally and stepped out into the bright cold
of a January afternoon. It seemed strange to find the sun shining after those hours of dark death within the hideout of the
Chief. About him, the suburban street on which he stood was
deserted. Trees rattled their skeleton limbs in the wind, but there
was no other sound. Even the chimneys of the houses about
him displayed no plumes of smoke and, looking more closely,
he saw that they were shuttered and closed. The explanation was
obvious. He was in some summer resort that had been closed
for the winter. The Chief had made an excellent choice. Nothing on earth is more deserted, more isolated and private than a
summer resort in the dead of winter.

WENTWORTH STRODE rapidly along the street. He
racked his brain to remember the sailing time of the *Picardie.*
Most of the major steamships he knew intimately, but this new
liner had not yet borne Richard Wentworth abroad. Already,
on its concrete pier, men and women might be whirling in the
throes of the Dancing Death! At the thought, the Spider broke
into a loping run. God, he must find quickly some clue to his

83

whereabouts… He rounded a corner and saw a neighborhood drugstore two blocks away, sprinted toward it. He thanked God that he had found money in his search through the enemy's house. Its presence in the purse that jounced against his groin was comforting….

He burst into the drugstore and a white-haired man rose heavily to his feet, shuffled forward peering over his glasses. He hesitated when he saw a man in Hindu garb stood before him. A scowl twisted his face.

"What do you want now?" he shouted. "Get the hell out of here before I call the police!" It was plain that he had had previous dealings with the men of the Chief. Wentworth saw that if he wanted swift action he would have to look elsewhere than to this man for information and help. He went past the druggist, wedged into a telephone booth which stood against the rear wall.

"New York Police headquarters," he told the operator. "And hurry. It's life and death."

The buzzing and faint voices on the wire continued for an eternity, it seemed to Wentworth. When the girl had put the call through, he shot quick questions at her. He was in South-ampton, he learned, far up the south shore of Long Island, and there was a seaplane port five miles to the south, or maybe it was the north, the operator wasn't sure. There was more delay while Wentworth dropped coins into the box and before the jangle of the bells had ceased he was barking crisp words into the transmitter.

"Kirkpatrick," he snapped. "Quickly. This is life and… Hello,

Kirkpatrick. The Spider speaking. Shut up and listen. The people behind the Dancing Death have a hide-out…" He ran swiftly through what he had learned and what threatened the *Picardie*. Even before he finished, Kirkpatrick was interrupting to snap orders at men he apparently had summoned to his office there at police headquarters in New York City.

"A half-hour before sailing," he told Wentworth. "You're sure it's the *Picardie?* The *Saxon Prince* is sailing, too."

"I'm sure…" Wentworth began, then broke off. It might have been a trick, that mention of the *Picardie*. It was clear that if Tarsa had not known when she first entered the room that he was behind the davenport, she had learned of it shortly afterward. She might well have misled him, thinking he might escape and wishing to give him misinformation… "I'm not sure," he snapped. "The information might have been given to mislead me. Better guard both boats. I'll be there as soon as I can make it. What is it?" Wentworth broke off in a bitter laugh. "When you find the hideout, you'll discover why the Spider serves the city better than your forces, Kirk. To hell with that…."

He snapped up the receiver, signaled the operator again and demanded a taxi, tried and failed to raise the airport. While he waited for the machine to arrive, he strode restlessly up and down the store, followed by the irate proprietor who shouted fiercely at him the entire while. Well Wentworth knew the danger of delaying here even to catch a taxi. Valuable as had been his service in warning Kirkpatrick, the Commissioner would not neglect to put men upon his trail at once. A swift call to police here at Southampton and they would be after him… Wentworth hurled from the drug store, stood rigidly on the corner waiting for the taxi. He saw it coming a great distance off and its approach seemed incredibly slow. The police would come at no such crawling pace. He flung into the cab.

"Get away from here fast!" he snapped.

THE DRUGGIST stood in the doorway, still reviling him. It would not do to let him hear that the destination was the airport nearby. The police would find that out soon enough when they got hold of the telephone operator… The taxi circled the block and Wentworth gave his directions, waved a ten-dollar bill at the driver.

"That's yours if you make the airport in less than ten minutes," he said, "and there's a dollar for each minute under nine that you clip off the time."

The taxi lurched forward with a lurch which sank Wentworth deep into the cushions. The *Picardie* sailed in half an hour. It would take ten minutes at least to travel the five miles to the airport. He had been able to raise no one there by telephone which meant that, even if there was a plane available, he would have to wait while it warmed up… The taxi made the airport in seven minutes, whirling Wentworth to the very door of the hangar and Wentworth banged on a locked door. Finally, he raced around to the ramp that sloped to the sea. A ship was there and a mechanic was puttering greasily beneath the cowling. There was no time for argument. Wentworth whipped out the automatic he had taken from Tarsa.

"Get down from there and start the engine," he ordered crisply.

The mechanic's face grayed beneath the grease, but he clambered down and tugged at the prop as Wentworth ordered. It took precious minutes to start the cold engine and it sputtered and rattled furiously as Wentworth tried to goose speed into the motor. With a gesture of the automatic he drew the mechanic aboard, into the cockpit before him. He could not risk a telephone call to the police which might send New York's flying cops into the air after him. He was going into the battle with the men of the Chief, and this time there would be no mistake when he killed.

The plane waddled down the ramp under the impetus of Wentworth's gunning took to the water with the motor still cold. The sea was choppy, white caps dotting the wave tops. Icy spume whipped into the Spider's face and his hands felt congealed on the stick. This was no weather for open cockpit flying without the very warmest of clothing... Over the waves, the cold-motored ship skipped. Wentworth did not dare lift it into the air yet, but at least he could put miles between himself and the shore by the time the engine warmed. Or he could if the seas beyond the out-licking spit of land were not too high. Within minutes, he saw that his fear was justified. The waves outside ran high and gray with flecks of white foam on their crests. There could be no take-off except in the harbor itself, and over there, on the shore, blue-coated men were racing around the hangar, shaking angry hands in the air. One man dropped to his knee with a rifle....

Well, there was no choice. The plane must take off, cold or not. Wentworth pivoted into the wind, yanked the throttle wide and rocked the ship over the choppy waves. He muscled the pontoons up on the step, skittered recklessly toward open water. If he failed to take off this time, it was likely there would be no second opportunity. The police had found the power boat that was used to service planes and were swarming aboard....

Motor roaring at full blast, the ship danced out of the comparative smoothness of the harbor and into the full threat of the seas. It was beginning to lift sluggishly but was as yet only inches above the water. There was a sloughing shock as a wave slapped the hull with its full gray weight. The plane staggered and Wentworth fought the almost overpowering impulse to attempt to muscle the ship upward. A too-steep climb now would spill him back in a whip-stall, wrecked hopelessly, would put him squarely in police hands....

A SECOND wave slapped the boat with less force, then the plane was up and sailing clear. The riflemen on shore sent a final bullet screaming after them and Wentworth was away, the wind on his port quarter, racing toward the city. The mechanic turned about slowly, his face white, his lips blue with cold. He clasped his hands before him and shook slowly, attempting a grin. Wentworth warranted congratulations after getting that ship off the water. The motor was nearly up to normal heat, functioning smoothly and the southern shore of Long Island raced past their starboard side. Without interference, Wentworth would reach the North River and the piers of the *Picardie* and the *Saxon Prince* in a half hour, and that would be fully fifteen or twenty minutes after they were due to slip their moorings. Of course, departures were not always on time, but in the big liners it was apt to be pretty close unless something unusual occurred. As Wentworth had heard the plans, it was intended that the *Picardie* should actually pull out into the North River and head southward. He devoted all his attention to jockeying the utmost speed from the seaplane. The motor was hammering at top speed and more than once he glanced up at the nacelle with its whirling propeller mounted above and behind him....

The Spider's hands were numb with cold. The scanty protection of the windshield could not keep the knife-edge of the wind from putting the frigid ache into his face, into his very eyeballs. The mechanic had crouched low in the cockpit snuggled under the curve of the cowling, but Wentworth had to sit erect. There was not only the matter of reaching the scene of the fight at the first possible moment by the shortest route, but there was the danger of interception by police or military planes....

His eyes had already picked out three close-flying specks that had lifted from behind Governors' Island. They might be taking mere practice flights or going to combat the killers, but there was an excellent chance that they were coming for him. He watched and the specks grew rapidly larger. There could be no longer any doubt. They were coming after the Spider!

Wentworth groped in the cockpit for the parachute pack he had noticed when he first entered. There was only one, but that would probably be *all* he would need. He pitched it forward into the cockpit with the mechanic and when the man lifted a startled face, Wentworth made a vigorous gesture over the side. It could not be mistaken, and, under the urge of a leveled automatic, the man fumbled quickly into his belts. By the time he was ready, Wentworth was flying over land. The wind would carry the man inland, rather than out to sea....

It took a significant, harsh gesture to make the mechanic bail out, but finally he leaped and was swept downward toward the earth. Probably the man would never believe it, but the Spider had done that to save his life. His plane was heavy and cumbersome compared with those of the three who pursued him, and they would carry machine guns. If Wentworth landed they would not fire. Otherwise, their deadly bullets would claw the seaplane to shreds. Wentworth's lips set grimly, in a smile. Well, he needn't concern himself with what would happen if he landed. He did not intend to go down... On the North River, the killers must already have struck, and, the Spider had a rendezvous there... with Death!

CHAPTER 9
THE SPIDER FINDS HIS FOE!

IF THE approaching army planes had any suspicion that the Spider had gone overside in the parachute, he soon undeceived them. The three ships swung above him and one dived past his nose, tripping his machine guns in a short burst. He zoomed, swung about in a vertical bank and coasted alongside the seaplane. He shook his balled fist at Wentworth and pointed downward to the water.

Wentworth knew that he presented a ludicrous picture. The turban had finally loosened under the whip of the wind and an end was streaming out behind him. His face was pinched with

The human missile struck the chest of the remaining Hindu!

cold and the woolen cloak that he wore about his shoulders, Hindu-fashion, was stained with blood. He looked toward the threatening pilot, smiled and shook his head. Then he steered calmly straight ahead.

The army plane swept up above him, dived on his tail and sent tracer bullets whistling through a wing. Wentworth did not even turn his head. He took his turban off and pitched it overside and it went down unraveling, whipping in the wind, reaching out for the shore. The plane pulled up above him. Wentworth hoped that they would think that the turban was a test of the wind preparatory to landing. If they did, he would gain a few minutes and each minute hurled him miles toward his goal in the North River. He would not be able to see the *Picardie* until he was almost above her because he was approaching the North River from behind the towers of Manhattan which already were lifting pointed fingers there ahead.

Wentworth was taking a desperate gamble. He would make no offensive move toward the army planes. He would not even dodge, but he would press resolutely on his way. He did not think that, in the absence of open hostility, those army fliers would shoot him down. To be sure, it was a system of warfare, to stalk an enemy unseen if possible, and bore him through the back. Wentworth himself had fought that way in the air over France, but this ship was unarmed. He did not think they would fire on him. If they did, it would be finish for the Spider.

A half dozen times, the army planes crowded about him, sending shots smoking near the seaplane but as Wentworth bored persistently on his way, they changed their tactics and grouped their ships closely about him. He was a prisoner under escort, and if he thought he could get away... From time to time, the pilots of the guardian planes glanced over at Wentworth, but they had given up the attempt to drive him down. Short of gunning him, they couldn't do it.

Manhattan wheeled past under Wentworth's pontoons and his eyes swept the North River. He spotted the *Picardie* with her two squat funnels almost immediately. She was pushing slowly down the river, had almost reached Bedloe's Island with its dwarfed Statue of Liberty. There seemed no unusual excitement going on about her; no boats followed her propellers' wake, and Wentworth swung sharply up the stream. The *Saxon Prince* berthed at Fiftieth Street, and....

Even as Wentworth whirled toward the German liner, he saw steam spurt upward from beside her funnels, saw the high stern push out into the river from her pier. He dropped lower, lower, with the army planes resolutely on each side of him, and before him. They made no more efforts to control his activities. At his present altitude, Wentworth would pass just above the masts of the *Saxon Prince* and he held his plane there while he peered anxiously toward the slowly moving ship. It had checked its backward drift and was threshing forward.... He could make out movement on her decks, see figures in black and white darting swiftly about. His jaw set in hard anger. Had his warning come too late to help the victims of the Dancing Death? Or what...?

AS HE darted even closer, a harsh curse rose in Wentworth's throat. Across the hurricane deck, a woman ran with her arms reaching out in frantic hopelessness before her. At her heels a bearded Hindu, resplendent in white from turban to feet, ran lightly. There were blotches of crimson on his clothing. As Wentworth saw him, the Hindu overtook the woman, caught her by the shoulder and whirled her about, drew back his knife....

Wentworth whipped his automatic out. It was madness to think that he could hit the man from his swiftly moving plane. The distance was too great for accurate shooting... But he aimed high and fired.

Whether the bullet whistled near, or whether it was the sound of the shot Wentworth did not know, but the Hindu's head jerked upward toward the ship. He hesitated with his knife and the woman jerked free and ran desperately forward again. She sprang to the railing of the ship and, while the Hindu reached for her once more, plunged into the sea....

Rage rose chokingly in Wentworth's throat. The girl was lost. Even if she survived the wash of the ship, the bite of its huge propellers, the cold would numb her into insensibility. Without thought of consequences, he whipped his seaplane into a sharp bank and went upwind again toward the *Saxon Prince*. He hoped that the army men in the other planes had seen what had happened there on the upper deck, that they would not attempt to interfere. One ship dodged frantically from his path and Wentworth cut the gun as he drifted nearer and nearer to the liner. What he was attempting was madness. He stood almost no chance of landing safely on the hurricane deck of the *Saxon Prince*, though the Spider was a consummate flier and before this had accomplished things that would have been certain death to many men. He was not acting blindly. The ship was moving in the same direction as his plane, the wind was in his face. Both those factors would tend to decrease the shock of landing, and he counted on crashing through some guy wires back of the funnels and thus absorbing additional impetus. Despite all that, he would land at a net speed close to thirty miles an hour. He took the chance willingly. It was his only chance of getting on the ship. The sides would be guarded by armed men of the Chief....

The army planes swung high, dived on him from over the liner and their machine guns belched a fury of hot lead upon him. One after another they circled and dived, three craft throwing death at the Spider. The pilots thought, of course, that he was behind the Dancing Death, that be was going to join his companions. That shot at the Hindu might have been interpreted as a signal... Wentworth could not dodge. He held the seaplane squarely on its course. He had to scrape past the cargo boom that raised its stub mast aft, slide in between that and the funnel... Bullets hammered a strut from the right wing. The shooting of the men was wild, frightened. They were afraid lest they drive lead into the *Saxon Prince*....

Losing altitude rapidly, Wentworth coasted in toward the deck. His eyes flicked back and forth from the funnels to the cargo boom. Damn! There was a guy wire stretched out to port which would snare his already weakened right wing unless he could....

Even as the alternative flashed through his brain, the right wing took the wire brace with its tip. The wing snapped off close to the fuselage of the plane, but the contact whirled its nose about toward the deck. The motor was already dead, the propeller barely spinning.

WENTWORTH HAD time for only one frantic thought, the motor in the nacelle above his head. If the ship pancaked, the motor would come crashing down through the cockpit… Frantically he yanked back on the stick, trying to spill the ship on its tail. The plane had turned a complete circle, its nose facing aft after the collision of the wing. The tail hit the hurricane deck, crumpled and the ship turned a backward somersault that brought its nose against the top of the funnel. The metal crumpled, Wentworth was thrown violently against his straps and the nacelle popped from its struts, crashed down and splintered the deck. But it had fallen away from Wentworth. His fingers were already fumbling with his straps as he hung upside down in the cockpit. The army planes were circling like angry wasps….

The hooks came unfastened and Wentworth plunged to the deck on his shoulders, stumbled to his feet with his hand groping for his automatic. It was gone, and there, racing across the deck toward him, were three Hindus with knives in their hands. His garb might fool them for moments, but they would soon detect the impersonation and then… Wentworth stooped to the deck. The plane had had a wooden propeller and it had smashed. He caught up one splintered blade and waited for the attack. The Hindus checked and one of them whipped an air pistol from his belt. Wentworth knew what that threatened—one of the darts of the Dancing Death! He lunged forward, the propeller fragment before his face. He had a fleeting memory of a dozen such charges he had made with the keen *tsurugi* in his fists and for a moment he longed mightily for that keen sword.

The air pistol coughed and Wentworth's hands twitched the propeller blade an inch to the left. It was sufficient. The dart struck the hard wood and quivered there and Wentworth was upon the three men before the air pistol could be cocked again. The blade swung once about his head. Its splintered end whipped across the face of one Hindu, thudded against the head and neck of the man with the gun. The first man reeled back screaming, hiding his mutilated face in his streaming hands, the second plunged to the deck with his head lolling limply, but the third Hindu seized his chance and leaped close with his keen knife raking upward for Wentworth's side.

It was a slim chance he had for escape, but he saw it instantly. If he checked his swirl with the propeller in an attempt to strike with it, he would receive that nine-inch blade between his ribs. If he spun on… He did that, deliberately throwing himself off balance in the hope of avoiding the knife. He felt it streak like fire across his side and knew that at least it had not gone home. With the momentum of his whirl, he brought the propeller blade circling again, caught the Hindu on the shoulder and spilled him to the deck. Before the man could rise, Wentworth dived on him with the splintered ends of the propeller held like a bayonet. The man quivered and lay still.

Wentworth stared about him. The deck was clear. Overhead, one plane still swung in a tight, fast circle and Wentworth hunted the other two ships. They were taking the water in the wake of the *Saxon Prince*, closing in….

THE PILOT circling overhead leaned over the edge of his cockpit and waved his open hand. He gestured toward the two ships behind, then to the aft rail of the *Saxon Prince*. No doubt as to his meaning. If Wentworth would clear the way, those three pilots would come aboard. They had seen his fight and understood that something more was happening here than they had anticipated. Perhaps the radio had carried them some message… Wentworth waved both arms in a wide circle, airplane language that signaled understanding, then he stooped over his victims. He recovered the air pistol, a quiver of darts and one knife. Then he ran swiftly to the after part of the hurricane deck Already, the third ship was circling to a landing with the other two.

Wentworth peered cautiously over the rail and choked on a curse. Horror was there on the deck below him. A woman dragged herself, screaming, on her arms, and the rest of her body was melting away under the fiendish torment of the Dissolver! A man pirouetted in the whirling grip of the Dancing Death while a group of terror-stricken prisoners huddled against the wall, forced to witness the atrocities. A half-dozen Hindus stood before them and at their feet they had spread out a silken cloth on which money and jewels lay in a glittering heap. Now one of the East Indians seized an aged man by the wrist and dragged him to his knees. He poised a tiny dart over the man's face… Looting—looting and murdering terribly—with the torture weapons to persuade their victims to disgorge. Heaven alone knew what had happened to the police, perhaps the Hindus had struck them also with the Dancing Death and the Dissolver. Even seasoned troops would flee before such torture.

There were six men there below whom the Spider must face with a single knife and a pistol which must be cocked and reloaded laboriously before each shot.

Wentworth whirled and raced back to the three men he had felled. The Hindu with the mutilated face had collapsed to the deck. Wentworth skipped him, caught up the man he had bayoneted with the propeller. He paused a moment to scribble in blood a Spider seal upon the man's forehead, then raced with him to the after rail.

He fired a dart into the face of the man who still was torturing the aged prisoner. Then he stood straight with the body of the dead Hindu poised high above his head.

"Death is among you!" he cried. "The Spider brings death!"

With the final word, he hurled the body straight at two more of the Hindus who already were pointing their deadly weapons upward. The corpse drove them backward to the floor and one of them tried to struggle to his feet. Wentworth stepped over the railing, poised a moment there with his knife between his teeth while he reloaded the torture gun, then he leaped to meet the three men who remained on their feet.

Instead of struggling to maintain his feet as he struck, Wentworth hurled himself into a somersault. Coming to his feet, he struck one Hindu in passing with the keen edge of the captured knife, ripped across his side. He snapped a dart into the face of a second man, and there were only two left to face, one just reeling to his feet from beneath the corpse Wentworth had hurled against him.

A KNIFE darted at Wentworth's throat. He caught the wrist,

whirled and had the man across his shoulders. He lifted the struggling, screaming Hindu straight above his head, gripping him by throat and thigh. Before him, another of the dark-skinned killers braced himself against the railing, dragging at a gun in his sash to supplement the knife that he already brandished. Wentworth set his shoulders, braced his legs and heaved the squirming Hindu straight at his fellow murderer. The human missile struck the chest of the remaining Hindu. There was a creaking, explosive snap as the railing gave way and both men pitched bodily outward into the wake of the ship. For a moment they were visible, bobbing above the surface. Then the white wash crimsoned. The propeller blades had done their work

Wentworth swung about, sending a searching glance over the deck. The Dissolver had finished the woman, but the man still whirled in the Death Dance. Wentworth strode to him, knocked him out. He left the two Hindus he had shot to twitch out their lives in screaming torture while be stared forward along the deck.

On other decks, there might be torture scenes, but at this point there was silence and triumph for a moment. He swung toward the water, saw that the three seaplanes of the army men were grouped close together, not fifty feet from the railing of the ship. He sprang to the bulwark, caught up life-buoys which were secured by lines and flung them overboard. He did not wait to see the army men catch them up and pull close, to see them clamber aboard. He swung to the cowering prisoners, some of whom were beginning to pluck up courage. To three of these he gave the guns of the Dancing Death, plucked from the bodies of the dead.

"See that those army men get aboard," he ordered tersely. "There are more darts in those pouches on the dead men. For the present, the reign of the Dancing Death is over."

One of the men dropped down on his knees. It was the elderly gentleman whom Wentworth had saved.

"Thank God, oh thank God, you have come, Spider!" he cried. "Now we are safe."

Wentworth paused for a moment, staring bitterly down into the twisted old face. Yes, in times like these people welcomed the Spider, but at all others they clamored for his death as eagerly as the Underworld whom he scourged. Wentworth's hard, firm lips twisted.

"You might tell the police about that," he said shortly. "Guard well, you three. If those army men get aboard, the fight is over." He strode rapidly away along the deck, reloaded the dart gun in his hand, bloodied knife tucked into his sash. His step was resilient and firm. He was very tired from his previous battle, and he had not escaped it completely unscathed, but he was still able to move and fight. That was all that mattered. The two top decks were cleared, but lower down, the carnage and the looting still went on, he was sure, and somewhere there he would find the Chief, in all his gory glory. When that moment came... Grimly Wentworth weighed the dart gun in his hand. The Chief should die by his own fearful medicine!

Wentworth whirled into a companionway, took the steps in two long strides, spun out on the deck. A guttural voice uttered a harsh curse and the Spider turned, gun hand rising. He looked into two fierce eyes which peered out at him through slits in a black hood, at a body encased from head to toe in a drapery of black. Exultation swam through Wentworth's body like fire. There were a dozen Hindus here, armed with guns and knives, but what did that matter? *The Spider was face to face with the Chief of the Dancing Death!*

CHAPTER 10
THE SPIDER MAKES A FRIEND

WENTWORTH'S RECOGNITION of the man before him and his action were simultaneous. He knew that he must strike swiftly if he were to remove the Chief before he himself was eliminated, but the dart gun was ready in his hand. He whipped it up, fired pointblank at the face behind the black hood. The man reeled, throwing up his hands, but the dart slid through his guard and Wentworth could see by the rigidity with which it quivered in the hood that it had struck flesh.

The Chief whirled, screaming, toward the rail and Wentworth ducked back into the companionway entrance. There was a sliding door and he whipped it shut, latched it and raced up the steps toward the deck above. He knew that the door would offer no real barrier to pursuit. It could easily be smashed and there were many other companionways between decks. He sprang out on the deck above and saw the turbaned head of a Hindu come into view over the rail. The man had taken the shortest route to the man who had killed their leader, up the stanchions of the railing. He was still too slow. Wentworth reached the point in a bound and the man plunged backward toward the water to escape the keen knife that flicked at his throat.

Wentworth stood by the railing, methodically reloading his dart pistol. Rather than exultant, he felt deadly grim. He had again wrought death amid the ranks of his enemies, but a dark doubt haunted him. The black-hooded figure in the Southampton den had been a fake. Might this one not also be a fake? Señor Madrigas was supposed to be in charge on the *Saxon Prince,* or so Tarsa had said. This hooded one had not moved with the lean agility of the Spaniard. Wentworth, dart gun ready, leaned far out over the railing and a violent curse squeezed to his lips. His guess was more than fulfilled. By the railing, on the deck below, two men held a third who was clad in a black robe. His hood had been whipped off and one of the two men was applying his lips to a wound in the cheek of the supposed Chief. It was not that which brought the oath to the Spider's lips, but the fact that this man in Chiefs clothing was only another Hindu. It wasn't possible that he was the Chief.

In a fury, Wentworth leveled the dart gun, sent a feathered harbinger of death into the nape of another Hindu. Then the whole group below whipped out of sight. He turned toward the rear, saw the army pilots climbing over the railing and take out automatics. He held up a hand palm-first in token of friendship and hurried to them, met their curious stares with direct gaze.

"There are more than a dozen Hindus on the deck below," Wentworth informed them rapidly. "God knows how many more there are. It looks as if all the Thugs in India had migrated here to murder and loot."

One of the three pilots stepped forward, presenting his automatic. "You are my prisoner, Spider," he said shortly. "Give up your weapons."

Wentworth waved a hand sharply. "All right, I'm your prisoner. Meantime, the passengers of this ship are being tortured and killed."

"We'll take care of them," the pilot announced coldly, his square jaw hard, his wind puckered eyes tightening. "Give up your—"

HIS VOICE choked off and a poison dart flowered from his throat. Wentworth whirled, flinging himself prone, whipping out his own dart gun. The Hindu with the bushy Sikh whiskers was crouched on the deck above, but before Wentworth could fire he had dodged from view. Two of the army pilots raced for the steep companionway leading upward. A coast guard patrol boat was casting a line with a grapple to the rail aft. Men in blue uniforms lined up on the deck with pistols strapped to their thighs.

Wentworth crossed swiftly to the pilot who had been shot and who was standing in the stupor that preceded the whirling agony of the Dancing Death. Wentworth plucked the dart from his throat and a woman screamed as he lifted his knife and gouged out the wound. He whirled toward a man standing nearby.

"Suck the poison from the wound and spit it on the deck," he said shortly. "It won't hurt you in your mouth."

The man came hesitantly forward, but when Wentworth cursed at him, he sprang to his task. A sharp burst of gunfire pulled Wentworth to the railing. The coast guard boat had sheered off again, was churning the waters in a frantic attempt at quick speed and a dark, low racer shot from under the port railing of the liner and streaked off toward the shore. In its wake raced four more. All of them carried the white-garbed figures of Hindus and, Wentworth knew, a heavy load of loot. He stood and looked slowly over the deck The work of the Spider was finished here as nearly as it could ever be finished anywhere. If he waited until the army pilots returned… He smiled slightly. He had no intention of waiting. He stooped, caught up the helmet and gun of the wounded pilot, strode to the railing.

"Hey!" called a man. "You're supposed to be under arrest."

"Sure," Wentworth told him grimly. He swung over the railing, sped rapidly down a line to the nearest seaplane. The pilots, having no way of starting the ships if they killed the motors, had left them ticking over slowly. Wentworth reached the cockpit, gunned the ship as the other two pilots raced back to the railing. Their flurried shots were seconds too late and Wentworth skipped the plane into the air. He waved an ironic good-bye, but he did not immediately flee. He skimmed at slowly increasing altitude over the water in the wake of the speeding pirate boats. They were incredibly fast, but the plane was still swifter. He made two murderous dives upon the crowded boats before his ammunition belts were exhausted. Then he swung up the East River.

Heavy weariness settled over Wentworth. The cold bit into his exhausted body and his wounds, slight though they were, began to throb in the symphony of fatigue that was claiming him. Though he knew his clothing would attract unwelcome attention, he set the plane down near a boat pier off Fulton Street, moored it with a light line and strode off without a word to the gaping loafers who cowered in the shelter of the warehouses.

In the cluttered streets of the East Side, he bought clothing and swiftly donned it. He had suffered serious losses in equipment, but he had several hundred dollars, thanks to his search in the hideout of the Chief. He caught a taxi to the hotel where he had taken a room, went with weighty stride to the elevator and upward.

His usually keen eyesight was veiled with his weariness and he failed to see that the house detective signaled the telephone operator and that she went swiftly to work at her board. He stumbled along and half fumbled the key into his door and stepped inside… A hand caught him on the shoulder and hurled him sharply forward, a gun muzzle gouged into his back.

"All right, Spider!" came the cheerful voice of Detective Bill Horace. "Do you want to give me your word not to escape again, or shall I put the cuffs on you?"

WENTWORTH WAS stunned out of his lethargy, and as Bill Horace himself had said, he had been made a detective too soon. There were many tricks of the trade that Horace didn't know. Wentworth lifted his right heel and set it solidly on the instep of Detective Bill Horace's foot. He whirled on it, slamming his elbow against the gun, following that up by a left to the jaw as he completed his turn. It was a simple trick, one that would never be worked on Bill Horace again, but this time it had served its purpose. Horace went limply against the side of the bed, bounced and hit the floor on his face, sprawling.

Wentworth stood crouched for an instant, then he straightened and shoved back his shoulders. It would be easy to walk out, but the Spider needed rest vitally. If Horace had found him at this obscure hotel, it was likely that many other such places were watched, too, and he could not afford to risk another run-in with officers. His reflexes were slowing… He handcuffed Bill Horace with his own manacles, seated him against the foot of the bed and linked the cuffs through a vertical rod. Then he revived the detective.

Horace opened his eyes blearily, pulled up his head with its tousled black hair. He grinned ruefully. "Well, I guess this means I go back to pounding the beat," he said, "unless I can persuade you to surrender."

Wentworth's heart went out warmly to the man. He was game, clean and game to the core. He smiled as he shook his head slowly. "Sorry, Bill, it's no go. However, I'll give you a chance. I've got to sleep and I'm going to do it here because I've got a hunch that all the other hotels are under watch, too. If you can figure a way to escape in the meantime, why you'll have me. Do you want to give me your word not to yell an alarm, or shall I gag you?"

Horace shrugged. "I'll give my word, Spider. You're right about the hotels being watched. I got photostats of your handwriting and had every hotel register in town canvassed to see if we could spot you. I was lucky enough to find the right hotel myself."

"Good work," Wentworth nodded. He yawned, stretched his aching body. "See you later." He flung himself down on the bed.

"Listen, Spider," said Horace, "why don't you give yourself up? I've got a hunch you can beat that case against you and this town's going to be too hot to hold you pretty soon otherwise. Every hotel will be watched for you and we're doing other things I can't tell you about. Surrender, before one of these mugs shoots you."

Wentworth said good-naturedly, "Shut up, Horace. I told you I was sleepy."

"Okay," Horace muttered, "I'll talk with you in the morning. Good night, Spider."

"Good night, Bill."

Wentworth had no way of knowing what time it was that he woke up, but he knew instantly what it was that had stirred him. Bill Horace was swaying the foot of the bed back and forth. At first, Wentworth thought that he was trying to loosen the foot of the bed so as to walk away with the handcuffs, but that would be ridiculous, of course, since it would drop Wentworth on the floor and arouse him. Then Wentworth saw that the door of the room was opening very slowly, an inch at a time. Wentworth had just time to recognize that the hunched outline of the man in the doorway was vaguely familiar, when the figure launched itself upon him and powerful fingers gripped his throat.

Wentworth's hand closed on his automatic and he brought it out, muzzle first. So fierce was the pressure on his throat that already his temples were beginning to pound and his neck ache from the bruising. His head was filled with sharp, shooting pains. But one bullet would fix that, blow this murderous fool off his chest… Wentworth was ready to shoot; then he recognized the man who was trying to kill him. It was Blackmon, the husband of the girl the Spider was falsely accused of having murdered. He couldn't shoot the man. Blackmon was innocent of any crime, was bent only on revenge. Wentworth jerked the gun free to slug with it. Blackness filled with fiery spots of red danced before his eyes. God above, if he didn't strike strongly and right the first time, he would never live to hit again! He struck with the gun… and missed… The weapon was terribly heavy. He couldn't even lift it to….

THROUGH THE dim blackness that was swarming over his brain, Wentworth heard a voice crying out. It was sharp and full of authority. The hands on his throat loosened a fraction and the voice came again.

"Blackmon, you're under arrest. Put up your hands and stand clear of the bed."

It was bewildering, that voice. It spoke of authority and yet… By God, it was Detective Bill Horace, handcuffed to the foot of the bed, who cried out. With the realization, Wentworth gathered his strength and, as the hands came clear of his throat, he struck again, hard and true, with the automatic. Blackmon thumped to the floor and Wentworth forced himself to his feet, stood swaying over the collapsed man. His voice rasped in a dry throat as he spoke:

"That was a good turn, Bill, I won't forget it."

Horace sighed. "Don't be a damned fool. If he'd killed you, he'd have been after me next. A murderer can't leave witnesses around loose."

Wentworth went down on a knee beside Blackmon. There was a grim smile on his lips. He couldn't help liking Bill Horace. Damnable always to have to fight the men he liked… Blackmon's pulse was slow but strong. He showed no signs of returning consciousness. Wentworth went to Horace.

"Blackmon's being here means that some of those devils with the poison dart guns are around somewhere," he explained swiftly. "It means they've traced me down. I've got to get out and I'm taking Blackmon with me. If you'll give me your promise to stay in the room here for ten minutes, I'll take the cuffs off you."

Horace laughed. Wentworth couldn't see his face in the darkness. "Why should I promise?" the detective demanded.

"Damn it, man," Wentworth swore, "don't you see that those killers would like nothing better than to kill you? I can't leave you here, helpless, to be butchered."

"I don't get you," Horace said slowly.

"Fool!" Wentworth raged, "Do you think Blackmon found me here without help when it took the entire police force of New York City to run me down? This is the second time Blackmon has tried to kill me, goaded on by the men behind the Dancing Death."

Wentworth snapped on the light, but kept clear of the window with its drawn shade, came back to face Horace. "Will you promise?" he demanded. "Every minute we delay here…."

Horace said slowly, "Very well. I promise to stay here in the room for ten minutes and not to give any warning meantime."

Without another word, Wentworth bent over, unfastened the handcuffs, strode to Blackmon and slapped a wet towel into his face. Detective Bill Horace stood looking at his back, his curly black head pulled forward a little while he absently chaffed his wrists. His forehead was frowning. It was hell to like a fellow as much as he did the Spider and still have to run him down. He suspected that his liking was part of the reason that Commissioner Kirkpatrick had assigned him to this job. Kirkpatrick rather liked the Spider himself... Horace blew out a slow breath.

"You mind if I get my gun? If those damned killers are apt to come here...."

BLACKMON WAS beginning to regain consciousness. Wentworth straightened, watched him toss his arms about. It was quite clear that he had saved this man's life with his prompt treatment of the dart wound, and because of that, he must flee again into the night which alone offered the Spider protection. He leaned over and slapped Blackmon hard across the cheek

"Get up," he ordered harshly. "Get up and take me to your masters."

Horace said, "Hey!"

"Your promise," Wentworth reminded him gruffly.

"Listen, Spider, it didn't apply to going after those guys. If you're going after them, I'm going too."

"I'll hold you to your promise," Wentworth said shortly. He leaned over and jerked Blackmon to his feet. The man lunged at him, made a grab for his throat and brought up against the wall when Wentworth's right drove in under his ear.

"You're going to promise to take me to your masters," Wentworth snarled, his voice low but intense, "or I'm going to beat the life out of you." He slapped Blackmon in the face again, and the man lunged at him. Wentworth's right drove in under the heart and Blackmon's head banged the plaster. "Where are they?" Wentworth demanded.

Blackmon's shoulders were broader than the Spider's and his body was hard and compact. There was no mistaking his strength and he should have been able to smash through Wentworth's guard and beat him down. The Spider had fought too many battles to allow him to get started. Not that the eventual outcome was in doubt, but there was no time. He slapped again with his body behind the blow.

"Fool!" he taunted him, "don't you know that these men you work for tried to kill you once—shot one of the darts which killed your wife, into your neck? If I hadn't torn it out and sucked the poison from the wound...."

Blackmon's shoulders were hunched for a charge but the Spider's words seemed to penetrate the haze of anger which blinded him. "You... did that?" he whispered.

"I did that. Now, will you tell where your masters are?"

Blackmon stood with his heavy arms hanging and pity stabbed to Wentworth's heart. The man was broken spiritually by the blow of his wife's murder. He could think only of avenging her, and that with his own powerful hands. He was not a brilliant man, never would have been if this blow had not fallen, but there was honesty in the broad openness of his face, and deep sincerity in his blue eyes. He lifted his hands slowly, closing them into knots.

"You're lying!" he said harshly, "Lying. You killed Elsie and tried to…" He pulled his head down and charged wildly. Wentworth stepped from his path.

"All right," he said. "You won't talk, I can see that. Don't force me to hurt you. Do you hear, you…?" A blow caught Wentworth on the shoulder and its power drove him back to the wall. He bounced out of the way, but Blackmon was deaf to his appeals. There was only one thing to do and Wentworth struck with the neatness of long experience. He stepped into Blackmon's charge, knocked aside a slashing blow and clipped his right hard to the point of the jaw. Blackmon went down and out. Wentworth stood looking down at him, his brave shoulders sagging a little. His breath was not quickened in the least. Absently he massaged his knuckles.

"That was a beaut!" Horace murmured at his elbow. "Man, could you teach me to hit like that?"

WENTWORTH TURNED, smiled at him wryly. Horace flushed, looked down uncomfortably, but his head came up. He looked directly into the blue-gray eyes that could glow with the cold murder fire of the Spider, but now were warm and quizzical.

"Look, Spider," he said, "I'm going to quit the force if you'll let me work with you. I know the wife would agree with me. You do more good in a week than the police accomplish in a couple of months, and I… Damn it, Spider, I *like* you!"

Wentworth shook his head. "I'm not married, Bill."

Horace frowned. "What has that got…? Oh, you mean that I am. But, hell, Tony wouldn't care. She…."

Wentworth clapped Horace on the shoulder, gripped his hand hard. "You're on the right path now, Bill," he said. "Keep it up and you'll be commissioner yourself some day. You keep calling me the Spider. I won't argue with you about that, because you're only echoing Kirkpatrick's beliefs. But I'll say this… The Spider would do everything in his power to keep another man from following in his footsteps…."

Horace bit his lip, looked down at the floor. "Listen, Spi… Mr. Wentworth. I'd like to tell you something, but it's a dead secret and I can't. I'll just say this. Go to police headquarters with me and surrender to Kirkpatrick. Please. See, Mr. Wentworth, I'm…" Bill Horace looked up and started. He was talking to a room empty save for himself and the unconscious figure of Eddie Blackmon stretched out on the floor. He sprang to the door, but with his hand on the knob, he stopped. A curse squeezed from his lips. For ten minutes he had to stay here. He drew his handcuffs from his pocket where he had placed them after being freed and thoughtfully locked himself to the head of the bed where he could reach the telephone….

"Police headquarters," he said flatly. Then: "Commissioner's office, please, Bill Horace speaking, Detective, second grade… Commissioner, Horace speaking. I had the Spider—or rather, Mr. Wentworth—a prisoner at the Chesterfield Hotel and he got away. I'm handcuffed to the bed here. Yes, sir, I can get away, but it isn't that I called up about. I want to resign. Damn it, I know that, Mr. Commissioner—beg your pardon, sir—but I can't fight a man as white as that. I…I might have to shoot him some time."

CHAPTER 11
THE SPIDER SURRENDERS

THAT CONVERSATION, if he could have heard it, would have brought a grave smile to Richard Wentworth's lips. He had an equal admiration for Detective Bill Horace… offering to throw over the job that was life and love to him, to risk his life in the hazards of the Spider. He'd have to pay Tony Horace a visit some time and tell her to watch out for that young man. He remembered Bill's wife well, remembered one night when she had held a gun on the Spider and talked wildly of murder because she believed he had killed her Bill….

Preoccupied as were Wentworth's thoughts, his eyes were keeping keen watch for him and now he checked his progress along the hall abruptly and threw himself close against the wall. He was not a second too soon, for with a hiss a feathered dart sped through the block of air which Wentworth's body a moment before had displaced. It slanted down from a transom above a door where the glint of light had betrayed to Wentworth that an assassin lurked in his path. He faded back along the wall until he reached the door next to the room from which the dart had been fired. A hand thrust out through the transom and another dart sped along the wall. It was fired blindly, but it narrowly missed accomplishing its purpose.

Wentworth was crouched in the doorway now and he listened

intently, ear against the panel, decided the room was empty and set to work with a lockpick hastily improvised from the pin of his belt buckle. A man who knew locks as thoroughly as Wentworth could manipulate these simple fastenings with anything strong enough to throw the bolt. Within fifteen seconds, he stepped inside the darkened room. He had no wish to invade the adjoining room and risk death. The killing of one more assassin of the Chief was less important than locating the leader's whereabouts. He listened at a connecting door, trying to search out the movements of the assassin. Now and again feet stepped softly across the floor, but that was all. Impatience stirred Wentworth. He was utterly worn out with the travail of the last day and his sleep had been broken almost at its start by Blackmon's entrance. Yet he could not desert this obvious trail. More important than any personal safety or comfort was the death of the Chief. The Spider settled himself to wait, to keep watch....

How much later it was, Wentworth did not know, but he came to himself with an abrupt realization that his long labors had taken toll of him and that he had slept. Furiously, he pulled himself to his feet, listened for movement in the adjoining room, but there was none. He manipulated the lock, opened the connecting door and cursed himself bitterly. He had lost the trail purely through exhaustion. However, he did not allow it to bother him long. Wentworth was not a man to fret over things past and done. He glanced out the window, saw that dawn was graying the eastern rim of the overcast sky, then set about making his toilet. Down the hall there a few doors, he could obtain fresh clothing from his suitcase, reclaim the garments of the Spider for which he had created a hiding place by making a false bottom in one of the drawers of the dresser. He could—if there was no police plant keeping watch. That was something he could not afford to chance.

Rapidly, the Spider stripped his hard body, examined the several knife gashes he had suffered in the battles with the Hindus. Already they were healing, thanks to the superb condition of his splendid system. He cleansed and bandaged them, tearing portions of the bed sheets. Then he went with swift vehemence through some setting up exercises and showered, afterwards punishing his browned skin with a coarse towel. Now if only he had clean linen... Wentworth shrugged, climbed into his clothes. His few hours sleep and the freshening of his shower had made him new again. He checked his single automatic—luckily he had got a supply of cartridges from his room the night before—then strode to the door. The hall was empty and he walked openly along it toward the elevator, past the door of the room where he had left Horace and the unconscious Blackmon. **WENTWORTH WAS** tingling with vitality, but strangely there was a depression of spirits for which he could not account. He knew what it portended. Always when danger pressed hard upon him, when the next corner might yield an assassin, his keenly attuned nerves thus gave him warning. Wentworth had long since ceased to puzzle over the reason for these queer premonitions and had come to accept them as being as bonafide as a gun shot. There was an explanation, of course. An animal soon learns to sense the presence of its enemies. Wentworth had lived through years in hourly danger of his life... Yet to save

117

him, he could detect no reason for the feeling today. He was not followed. The elevator boy did not glance at him curiously, and yet… and yet….

For that reason, Wentworth was unusually alert as he strode from the cage and angled across the lobby toward the main doors of the hotel. He noticed what otherwise might have escaped his attention. There were two men in chauffeur's uniforms idling beside glossy limousines beside the door. There were two reasons why that caught his attention immediately. This was a cheap hotel where owners of cars of that sort could have no business, and it was only seven-thirty in the morning, a curious hour for the wealthy to be abroad.

Wentworth checked his approach to the door as if a sudden idea had occurred to him, turned and glanced about the lobby. There was a restaurant attached to the hotel and he nodded his head, strode into it. The place was scantly occupied so early in the morning. Wentworth ordered a large breakfast, recalling that he had not eaten in many hours and settled himself to a leisurely meal. He had a seat where he could watch the two simulated chauffeurs. Presently, one of them drove away and a short while later, the same limousine reappeared with a new driver and the other "chauffeur" duplicated that performance. Wentworth's suspicions were confirmed. Those two were keeping watch over the hotel—whether police or servants of the Chief, Wentworth did not know—but that need not concern him. He finished his breakfast, attached himself to a group leaving the now well-filled restaurant and strolled unhurriedly away. He had not been spotted, but the incident had served to show him the carefulness with which he was being hunted. He passed two other hotels on the street and both of them had watchers, Wentworth's discerning eye ascertained. He frowned. Was this going on all over the city, or was it merely this street that was being kept under surveillance?

At the corner, Wentworth purchased a newspaper. There were screaming headlines about the disaster of the *Saxon Prince* as they called it. Those dead on the liner itself numbered forty-six. On the pier, twenty-five policemen had perished under the torture of the Dancing Death and the Dissolver, along with some sixty others of both sexes. The loot—the personal losses were incalculable—but the liner's strong box had been robbed of over a million dollars in gold. Wentworth forced himself to read these things before he turned his attention to the headline that was searing into his brain:

Spider Kidnaps Wife of Nemesis!

There was a reproduction of a letter warning Detective Bill Horace that unless he ceased his efforts to capture the Spider, Horace's wife would be tortured to death! Wentworth kept himself under rigid control while he read the details of how Tony Horace had been lured from her home by an early morning call saying her husband had been wounded by the Spider—how a policeman on the beat had heard her scream and seen her snatched into a sedan while her brother, who had been spending the night at the house, was knocked insensible and left lying on the sidewalk. It had been as simple as that.

HORACE HAD been removed from duty by Commissioner

Kirkpatrick, but had refused to quit the job. "I'll get the Spider, with or without my badge," he had told the reporters. "I had him a prisoner last night and he impressed me as a white guy. I guess he was just pulling the wool over my eyes. I'll get him now and I'm serving notice on the Spider that I'll come shooting...."

Wentworth stared at the page before him with hard, embittered eyes. Surely, Horace couldn't actually believe the Spider had kidnapped his wife. There must be some trickery about it somewhere, perhaps an attempt to lure Wentworth into a trap. Wentworth was moving heavily down the garish width of daytime Broadway. His fists were knotted in his pockets, but he was not so preoccupied that he did not see men watching two more hotels. One of the watchers turned narrowed eyes upon Wentworth and for a moment half-recognition flared there.

Only by a strenuous effort did Wentworth manage to keep himself from quickening his pace. He even paused at the corner to allow an automobile to pass and each second he thought to feel a hand close on his shoulder. Most men would have turned to look back at the detective and would have confirmed the suspicion that was burgeoning there, made sure of their arrest, but Wentworth kept himself rigidly in hand and strolled on down Broadway—and the danger passed.

Wentworth tried to force his mind to the task before him, but it strayed obstinately back to the fact that Bill Horace who last night had been ready to sacrifice his career to help the Spider now believed him guilty of kidnaping his wife and holding her hostage to turn him from his duty. He entered a subway with no clear idea in his mind except the need to think over his position, turned to the paper again. Quotations from Kirkpatrick were there in the headlines:

> The Spider must be hunted down like the mad dog he is… Every resource of the New York police department is being turned to that one task; every hotel is being watched—every tourist camp, all entrances to the city. Lodging houses are being regularly patrolled and new tenants of apartment buildings checked. Once and for all, we must end this menace to humanity….

Wentworth's lips were hard against his teeth. Nowhere in any of the stories was there any mention of the heroic part he had played yesterday aboard the *Saxon Prince*. His presence was mentioned, but only as leader of the murderous Hindus. Kirkpatrick was being very careful that no atom of credit revealed the truth to the public. How could Nita lend herself to any such falsification of fact? She knew, must know, that he had no hand in the horrors of the Dancing Death, and yet she kept silent while Kirkpatrick and his men hounded him with drawn guns… Bitterness assailed him. He stared unseeingly at the newspaper which brought him this devastating information. Loneliness and doubt overwhelmed him. It was a rare thing that the Spider's resolution should waver, that he should for a moment doubt the wisdom of the course he pursued. But the woman he loved and trusted and the man who was his sincerest friend, had both turned against him in his extremity. The rustling of his paper penetrated his consciousness and he realized that his hands were shaking. The hands of the Spider trembling!

He threw back his head and laughed and the subway guard, leaning against the steel door frame, looked at him curiously, then shuffled off to open the doors as brakes squealed for a station. Wentworth rose and promptly left the train, but when it had gone, he stood for a long while looking at the empty tracks....

THE SPIDER went to the street and absently took a taxi whose driver signaled for attention. He glanced about him as the man turned, hand on the meter flag, to ask his destination. A street sign read *181 St. W.* Bill Horace's home was near here, on Washington Terrace. Wentworth's face hardened with resolution, and he gave Horace's address.

He sat woodenly, then, while the taxi droned along the half-empty streets of mid-morning. With Nita's constant trust, with his comrade-servants beside him, he had never before realized how necessary it was to him that some one should believe in him. Now that they had been torn away... He looked down at his hand, clenched hard about the newspaper, and for once in his vigorous life, self-doubt arose to assail him. How many years was it now since first he had donned the valorous garments of the Spider? What sort of man had he become? But he knew without introspection. He was a man to whose hand a gun was more familiar than the handclasp of a friend, whose life was spent amid horror and death, whose eyes could never gaze upon a fellow man without probing behind the mask of humdrum existence and wondering: Shall I some day be forced to kill this man? If some one looked at him steadily or curiously, as had that guard upon the subway, he must immediately think that they had recognized him for what he was, that he was in peril of death or arrest through the agency of the person who looked. All this, merely that he might serve an ideal of justice. Oh, there had been personal reasons behind his initial foray beyond the law—a dear friend was being framed out of life and honor and home. And there had been the example of his father, who had died when Wentworth was scarcely in his teens, a great lawyer murdered by criminals because he had dared defy them to save an innocent man they had made their scape-goat.

Wentworth thought fleetingly of these things and the words that Nita had uttered—God, it was centuries ago—came back to haunt him. Hadn't they suffered enough? Was there to be, then, no reward? It was a weary road he traveled, and lonely… lonely.…

"Here you are, sir," the taxi driver said and Wentworth came to himself with a start, saw that the door of the cab stood open and realized that the machine must have been stationary for a minute or more. He alighted before a yellow-brick apartment building which reared its blank face five stories above the street. He paid the driver and walked into the building, peered at the names above the mail boxes. William R. Horace, he saw, had apartment 5C. That would be the fifth floor and it was a walk-up building.

It was madness, Wentworth knew, to approach Horace's apartment thus openly. Probably the detective would not even be home, but Wentworth was quite sure that Kirkpatrick would have the place watched. Whatever he said to the newspapers, he would not believe that Wentworth had kidnaped Tony Horace.

Kirkpatrick could gauge the workings of Wentworth's mind to a nicety, too, and would know that he would want to see Horace—to persuade him that what seemed true was not. The men of the Chief, also, might well keep watch here.

Wentworth smiled bitterly to himself as he climbed the endless short flights of steps toward the fifth floor. Somehow all that did not matter. What did matter was the fact that Bill Horace believed him guilty of kidnaping his wife. He reached the fifth floor and his hand reached out for the bell. Then he hesitated. He could hear a woman's voice inside the apartment and somehow its accents were strangely familiar. They sent tingling memories over his body. Nita! Nita van Sloan was in that room… Wentworth shook his head. He was suffering from hallucinations brought on by melancholia. He rang the bell and the voices stopped, a man's feet moved heavily to the door, opened it.…

BILL HORACE stood staring at him. Then his shoulders moved heavily and he stepped back with a wan smile and made way for Wentworth to enter.

"Come in, Spider," he said, "Your advocate came first."

The door opened wide and in the hallway Wentworth beheld Nita van Sloan. He started forward, then checked his eager stride and stood, coldly sure of himself, his head lifted with that old arrogant poise which Nita knew so well. The door closed suddenly behind him.

"I came to tell you, Horace," he said slowly, weightily, "that I did not kidnap your wife." His eyes burned into Nita's, and his heart was beating suffocatingly in his throat. He had not realized how terribly he had missed her, how his arms had ached for the softness of her. His tongue touched his lips. "Is Kirkpatrick really such a fool as to think I did? Does he believe that I am behind this Dancing Death?"

Nita had started forward with a glad cry on her lips when she saw Wentworth, but his glance had frozen her. She stood, very pale and straight, not two strides away in the hallway where doors opened on the neat orderliness of Tony Horace's living room and upon a kitchen that glistened with white and red. Her violet eyes had smudges of shadow beneath them and they burned, burned into her lover's face. Horace said dully, "I don't know about Kirkpatrick. I don't believe you kidnaped Tony. Those reporters got me when they'd just told me what had happened. I was… was excited. After I'd thought a bit, I knew you couldn't have done it. I was telling Miss van Sloan here…."

Wentworth smiled with stiff lips. "If Kirkpatrick believes…" He stopped, dragged a hand heavily across his forehead, pushed numb fingers against his eyes. Then he dropped his hand, stood very straight. "I have always done what I believed best for the common good. If Kirkpatrick is pursuing me to the exclusion of fighting those devilish Hindus, then…" He swallowed hard, laughed bitterly, lifted his shoulders in a shrug. "Get your coat and hat, Horace, and take me to headquarters."

Nita took a stumbling step forward, her hands clasping, her face lighted by an incredulous joy. "Oh, Dick, do you really mean you'll surrender? I'm so glad… so glad…" She bowed her face into her hands and wept to show how glad she was.

Horace said heavily, "I'll go with you to headquarters, sure.

He plunged toward the car, while things spun crazily....

But I can't take you in. I turned in my badge last night after you left me in the hotel. Commissioner Kirkpatrick wouldn't accept it, but he can't make me serve if…."

A key rasped in the lock and the door behind Wentworth was thrown violently open. "There he is!" shouted a young, keen voice. "There, the Spider. Kill him. *Kill him!*"

Wentworth whirled. A young man was pointing at him with an extended arm which trembled and behind him were four police officers with their revolvers in their hands….

CHAPTER 12
NITA LENDS A HAND

WENTWORTH LOOKED calmly into the faces of the armed police and a question flashed through his mind as to whether Horace had known they were on the way and had deliberately detained him. Curiously, it was this, rather than how he could escape from his dilemma, that entered his mind. He was inclined to believe that Horace was not involved. He smiled at the police.

"I would advise you not to shoot," he cautioned pleasantly. "You might hit innocent persons."

The metal door had almost hit him when it swung open. It was necessary to move his left hand only two inches to touch its edge and he slammed it shut with an emphasis that abruptly brought shoulder and his whole body into play. He followed the flip of his hand by ramming his shoulder home against the panel. The door slammed hard, his hand found and fastened the bolts. He whirled toward Horace, who shook his head slowly as if denying that he had any part in the arrangements.

"Why try to get away," he asked, "if you're planning to surrender?"

Wentworth laughed harshly at he went past Horace. "It's one thing to surrender and another to be hauled in. Do you think they'd believe I was planning to surrender? I…" He choked off his words as window-glass crashed in the living room. Nita's hand caught his arm.

"Please, Dick," she whispered. "Don't try to get away. They'll kill you…."

Wentworth whipped his arm clear, leaped back beside Horace and snapped his fist cleanly to the detective's jaw, then he bolted past the kitchen door, ducked into what he saw was a bathroom. It was more likely to have a lock… Yes, there it was. He threw it, crossed the room in a stride and threw up the window. It had been necessary to protect Horace from a suspicion that he was harboring the Spider and knocking him unconscious had taken care of that. Nita… Well, her position with Kirkpatrick was too well known for her to be suspected. The thought was bitter in Wentworth's mouth. He thrust it from him… That crash of glass in the living room had betokened the entrance of a policeman by the fire escape. It would have a ladder to the roof, where Wentworth was going, but perhaps the man would not think of that in time to prevent him.

A knock thundered on the door. "Open in the name of the Law," a man mumbled. "Open, or we'll shoot you through the door."

Wentworth sent his mocking laughter toward them. "Come ahead, Law," he called, "and come shooting." He ducked outside the window then, straightened and groped for the projection of the eaves several feet above his head. If they would only shoot, it would drown any noise he might make... Ah, there it was. Bullets hammered through the door and he slid down the window, hoping to baffle them for a few moments. He got his fingers tentatively on the eave and straightened, clinging to the frame of the window....

The tin that covered the eave was icy cold and Wentworth's fingers were already numbing. He must be quick for more reasons than one. If police guessed what he was doing, it would be the work of an instant to tumble him five stories below to the cement floor of this air-shaft. Cautiously, he freed his other hand, clawed his fingers over the edge of the eave and, clamping his teeth hard, cautiously allowed his body to swing out into space. As his fingers took the strain, Wentworth began instant swift action. He was too wise to attempt to get his palms immediately over the eaves. For the present, his fingers would hold better, but as he hung, his back was to the wall of the building. Either he must bring up his legs, muscle himself straight upward and allow his knees to rest on the ledge outside the roof balustrade, or he must turn about, moving one hand at a time until his face was toward the wall and then muscle himself upward. The latter would be easier, once his hands were reversed, but meantime, there was the necessity of dangling by one hand at a time for a space of seconds....

WENTWORTH HAD already made his choice and he

began to act immediately. Using his cautious swing to help, he flexed his arms, drew his legs up. His forehead pressed against the under side of the eave and he used that as a lever to speed his acrobatics. He bent at the waist, pushed his legs straight up, tried to curl over to get his knees on the roof, after which the rest would be easy. Despite the cold that whipped through the air shaft, his face beaded with sweat. His breath panted out in exhausting gasps. All feeling had gone from his fingers long ago, but there could be no fresh grip. There was a heavy crash in the bathroom he had left—was it hours or only brief seconds before?—and then another crash. Wentworth's face pressed against the eave now. He pulled his head back so that his shoulders could bear the pressure, tried blindly to pull his knees down toward the eave. It would have to be soon, damned soon, or it would be too late. One of his hands slipped a fraction of an inch. His arms were near the breaking point. This was no feat for a man in an overcoat. It was difficult enough when the hands had a firm grip on a trapeze and the acrobat was clad in light gymnasium clothes.

There was a final crash within and the door slammed wide, two men catapulted into the bathroom. Luckily the glass of the window was opaque. That gave Wentworth a few brief seconds while they grasped the meaning of the empty bathroom. Desperately, he expended the final atom of his energy, felt his knees touch the level above. The feat was not finished yet. Most of his weight was still below the level of the eave, but at least he could ease the strain upon his hands by partially supporting his body up there. He bore down heavily on his knees. His thighs were fully supported now. He had only to wriggle backward until it was his waist—rather than the thigh joint—was on the edge, reverse the position of his hands and he could raise his body from that perilous suspension....

With a crash, the bathroom window was flung open. A policeman thrust out an irate face, gun beside his cheek. He pointed it upward to where Wentworth struggled.

"Surrender, damn you!" the policeman shouted. "Come back here!"

Despite his perilous position, his utter exhaustion, Wentworth gasped a laugh. *Come back here!* He had got his hands in the final position now, laughed again.

"I'm afraid... coming back... would be impossible."

He ducked back over the verge as the gun blasted. Lead chipped across the edge where a moment before his head had dangled, another bored upward through the eave. Wentworth caught the balustrade and climbed clumsily over. Ordinarily, he would have vaulted it easily... Below him, a man's hoarse shout was sounding. He could not hear the footsteps, but he knew that police were rushing for the fire escape which would bring them to the roof. Wentworth flung a swift glance about. There were three apartment buildings in a row, their roofs virtually on a level. He was on the central one, but there was no time to run forward to the place where the roofs joined. The air shaft beside which he stood was fully sixty feet long. Wentworth laughed giddily. The excitement of the chase was upon him. He could leap the air shaft, or he could face the police. He flung off over-coat and hat, tossed them into the air shaft, then darted toward the kiosk covering the steps leading into the apartment house where Bill Horace lived. He reached it only a second before the door slammed open and policemen poured out. Others had topped the balustrade there where the fire escape ladder hooked upward. They lunged toward the spot where Wentworth had climbed upward, peered over, saw the overcoat and hat spraddled on the pavement far below. Did they take it for a corpse?

Wentworth had counted on that, hoped that it would fool them for a hair-breadth of time at least. He whipped inside the kiosk, pulled the door shut and locked it. A gun crashed and lead whipped past within an inch of his head. He laughed again, took the steps downward with great leaping strides. The door of Bill Horace's apartment swung agape. The young man who had led the police was bending over Bill Horace. Nita van Sloan stood with a gun in her hand, facing toward the living room.

FOR A moment there on the landing, Wentworth hesitated, looking at Nita's proud figure. She was leaning forward, taut with eagerness or anxiety. She must have felt the pressure of his loving eyes for she turned abruptly, saw Wentworth.

A smile curved her lips, her hands reached for him, then Wentworth whirled and was gone. There was no longer laughter on his lips.

Nita could love him like that—he had seen the joy in her face at his escape—she could come to Bill Horace to plead his cause and yet she had thrown in with Kirkpatrick. She had betrayed him. Wentworth shrugged aside the thought. There was no time for useless regrets. He reached the street. There were three police cars there, one cop guarding them. As Wentworth sprang to the curb, a voice shouted from above.

"The Spider! Kill him!"

The uniformed policeman was already reaching for his holstered revolver, but he was seconds too slow. Wentworth hit him running, hurled him to the pavement, bent to slug him into unconsciousness. He straightened. One car which the cop had guarded had the key in the ignition lock. It leaped into motion at a touch and Wentworth sped off with lead hailing down from above. He could not go far like this. The cold bit into his scantily protected body, a police car driven by a civilian would attract attention....

A half block from Broadway, Wentworth abandoned the car, walked into a clothing shop to get a hat and coat. The need of the purchase angered him. To be sure, he still had some of the money he had taken from the men of the Chief, but to have to spend them for things like this... The salesman was staring at him curiously. As Wentworth waited for his change, the man glanced at his face, and then once again. His own countenance drained of all color and his hand, reaching out with the money, was shaking so that he could scarcely move the fingers. There could be no doubt that the broadcasting of Wentworth's picture in the newspapers had caused him to be recognized. There was nothing to be done about it. Wentworth stalked from the store, heard the salesman snatch up the telephone.

"The police! Quick! The police...."

Wentworth turned the corner and entered a taxi cab. "The subway station," he said. "Quickly, I'm in a hurry."

Behind him, he heard a shout, "The Spider! I seen the Spider. He went down that way…" It was the salesman again. The taxi driver turned a white face about. Wentworth parted his lips in a thin smile.

"I said quickly!" he prompted.

The taxi driver whipped to the front, snapped the cab into gear and shot it forward. Wentworth turned on the radio in the cab, dialed to police signal wave lengths and heard the carrier wave-signal sound. The announcer's usually cut and dried voice was excited.

"Car three-forty-two, car three-four-two. Go to thirty-six-hundred-and-five Broadway… Spider seen there. Just bought a dark blue overcoat, belted back, a black felt hat… Here's something later. He took a yellow taxi at the corner of one-eighty-first and Broadway, headed east…."

Wentworth called to the driver, "Are we going east?"

The driver stammered, "N-n-no, sir," and whirled the cab southward and then west. The quavering wail of a police siren crescendoed out of the south. The radio director was busy sending more police cars to pursue the Spider. Wentworth halted the taxi at a subway station, took the driver with him to a train and put him aboard, then headed for the steps. A few moments later, he boarded another train headed in the same direction. When he passed the next station, be saw the taxi driver in one of the telephone booths talking furiously, with gestures….

POLICE WOULD cover the subway in both directions, of course, but they would be inclined to think he had headed downtown since he had sent the taxi driver in the opposite direction. Wentworth got off at the next station after the one at which he had seen the driver, took a taxi at the surface and directed the driver to take him to Pelham Manor. During those exciting moments of the chase, he had made a momentous decision. It was impossible any longer to battle against the men of the Chief and at the same time dodge the police. The Spider had done it before, but that had been when he had the full resources of his millions and the help of his able comrades, Jackson and Ram Singh. Besides that, there never had been such a wholesale organization of police against him as Kirkpatrick had assembled. He was terribly handicapped and there remained only the course of action he had planned. He was going to see Kirkpatrick, and if he could not force him to turn his forces to the defeat of the Chief, then he would... well, kidnap Kirkpatrick!

It was the Commissioner who was the heart and soul of the attack against him, Wentworth knew. With him out of the way, there would be no more of this falsification of events to twist the entire mad battle into a *jihad* against the Spider. With Kirkpatrick out of the way, the Spider could once more turn his whole attention to the Chief. Possibly, he might avail himself of Bill Horace's offer to help. Surely, now, police would not look for the Spider again at Horace's place.

It was a long, tedious ride to Pelham Manor, across town on Mosholu Parkway, then hacking along the Shore Road. It was blustering with cold winds and there was more than a promise of snow in the overcast sky. Wentworth did not think that Kirkpatrick would be home at his ancestral place in Pelham Manor, but sooner or later, when the furor of the chase for the Spider died out, he would return there to rest. And when he did, the Spider would be waiting for him....

Before attempting an entrance, Wentworth had the cab driver roll past the big house which sat in remote dignity behind head-high hedges of boxwood. There were two policemen in uniform at the outer gate, two more on the porch... Wentworth shook his head and ordered the driver to take him to a nearby subway station, left the cab there. He had no intention of abandoning his attempt, but with that force on guard, it would have to be done by night. The darkness had long been the Spider's friend and it would have to serve him once more....

Wentworth ate a leisurely lunch of miserable food in a restaurant he stumbled across, spent the short winter afternoon in a motion picture theater where he saw not one bit of the picture. Afterward, he rented a speedy sedan from a Drive-It-Yourself company and parked it carefully a block from the home of Stanley Kirkpatrick. Then he walked briskly along through the darkness, hands shoved deep into his pockets, coat collar turned up about his ears. The snow had already begun to laze down through the night, weaving a moving curtain like gauze about the street lights, laying a white film upon withered grass and hedges. It was much warmer and the night was very still.

It was unlikely that anyone would be looking for him here, but Wentworth nevertheless disguised his manner of walking. Head and shoulders were no longer erect and there was nothing crisp about his stride. He checked curiously once when he saw an automobile with a caravan trailer behind it parked at the curb just ahead. It seemed a peculiar thing to see on this tree-shadowed street. There were hundreds of such camping trailers, Wentworth knew, and of course there was no reason why one should not be parked just at this place. His momentary hesitation was no more than a shuffle of feet and he went steadily ahead, striding past the caravan with no more than a sideways glance. There was only the parking light burning and no one seemed to occupy either automobile or trailer. Wentworth stalked on with his brows frowning in thought. That trailer would provide a splendid means of kidnaping Kirkpatrick, if he could avoid having suspicion attached to its being in the neighborhood. While it provided excellent means of concealment, it also was conspicuous and it would hamper swift movement....

WENTWORTH STEPPED across a street whose film of snow was as yet unbroken by tracks and was beside the black hedge which encircled the block occupied by Kirkpatrick's home. The police guards would still be there, of course. His only chance was to force Kirkpatrick to stroll casually out with him, as though for a walk in the snow. A guard would accompany them, of course, but it would be a small matter to overpower one guard as opposed to the half dozen or so who were about the mansion.

Headlights flamed abruptly down the street he had just traversed and he crowded close against the hedge, threw a swift glance over his shoulder. Either the auto with the trailer behind it had just started up or some other car had turned the corner... There was no time for speculation. Wentworth ducked through the close branches of the hedge at a spot he knew and, keeping in the shadow of the boxwood, sent his keen eyes probing the darkness of the shrub-dotted slope which reached up to the house itself.

There were lights in a few windows, but mostly in the servant quarters, so that Wentworth guessed that Kirkpatrick was not yet home. He left the hedge, crept from shrub to shrub as he made his way rapidly uphill. There was a certain basement window which he had entered before, through which he could gain ingress to the house. He would go to Kirkpatrick's study and wait there… With no warning at all, a dozen floodlights blazed out from the roof of Kirkpatrick's mansion, coating the grounds with silvery light. Even the shadows of the shrubbery were invaded by the reflection on the falling snow so that the yard became gilded more brightly than by a full moon. Simultaneously a half dozen policemen darted out from the shadows of the mansion, from other clumps of shrubbery, and raced in his direction. Wentworth cursed under his breath. He did not fight police, had never fired a harmful shot at an honest officer. It seemed quite plain that either through some signal system or secret surveillance, he had been spotted in his passage through the hedge. Whether or not they knew who he was, there was no way of telling, but they came racing with guns in their fists. Certainly, Wentworth could not delay to parley with them. Every racing second brought him nearer to danger… Nor could he conceal himself against that light and the search that was sure to follow it if he were not spotted immediately.

Wentworth whirled, crouched low, ran frantically for the cover of the hedge. He was not seen at once, but before he had taken a dozen strides, a man shouted a command to halt and a gun blasted, its sound queerly muffled by the snow. Wentworth had only one thing in his favor, the lighting and the falling snow made aim an uncertain thing. He could see that one policeman, near the hedge, was sprinting to cut him off, gleams of light flashing from his gun as his arms pumped.

He had been a fool to attempt this invasion, Wentworth acknowledged to himself. He had done more daring things in the past, but always Ram Singh or Jackson had been waiting nearby with a car, ready to snatch him from danger. Now he must run a full two blocks, start the motor of the car. He hit the hedge at full sprint, missed the exact spot of the passage by which he had entered, recoiled and tried again. The second time, he found the place but the policeman had gained a good fifteen feet. He was near enough already to shoot with considerable accuracy. Why didn't he…?

Wentworth scrambled through the hedge, slipped as he hit the snow-coated sidewalk and nearly fell. He was aware of an automobile there against the curbstone, of its headlights streaming through the darkness.

"Dick! Dick! Into the car…!"

WENTWORTH RECOGNIZED that voice with a gasp that was both joy and surprise. Nita! Good God, how had she come to be here? He changed direction again, sprinted for the car which already was rolling slowly ahead. It stopped and Nita stepped into view… Behind Wentworth the hedge crashed to the assault of a man's body. Now he could hear what had been hidden from him before, the slap of a man's feet on the sidewalk as a policeman raced toward him from the next street. The snow had masked that. Danger and death were very close, but a strange elation was throbbing through Wentworth's body. Nita had come to his assistance. That meant that the days of cruel misunderstanding were over at last, that they would fight together again, side by side....

"Nita!" Wentworth exulted. It seemed to him that he cried it aloud, but it was a whisper, of course. If he were to escape, there must be no name shouted into the night to betray them. He reached out his arms as he sprang across the narrow strip of grass toward her. In the snow reflected light, he could see the anxious smile on her lips, greeting him, and fearing for him at the same time. He saw her mouth open in a sudden scream of terror.

"Duck, Dick," she cried. "Duck...!"

Wentworth started to dodge, then he saw from the way she stood, from the direction of her gaze that if he jumped aside, Nita would be directly in line with the police gun which undoubtedly was leveled at him from the break in the hedge. He sprang mightily toward the car, only a few feet away now, and a great fist punched him in the back and helped him along. He saw Nita's hands reaching for him, saw her mouth open, but he could hear nothing save a vast thundering that became a roar within his head. Things spun crazily. He couldn't see Nita any longer, but he was stumbling, stumbling, hands were on him. A gun blasted close at hand and then, seconds later, that huge, cruel fist struck him again... He knew that he threw back his head and the impulse to laugh stirred in his soul, but he heard nothing. That was the greatest mockery of all. He had found

Nita again after all these weary hours of death and now police guns, police bullets… He heard the laughter now. It was gasping, hollow, mirthless. It exploded something in his breast and red fire reeled out in waves. Strangely, it came from within his breast and yet he could see it with his eyes. It flickered and died and the blackness was deep and, thank God, painless….

CHAPTER 13
AGAIN, CORPORAL DEATH

I T WAS queer to come back from death and find yourself under yards and yards of black silk like this. Wentworth fought his way upward, peeling bolts of silk from in front of his eyes, from off his brain. The silk became, by imperceptible stages, mere darkness, and after an infinite time, Wentworth opened his eyes. The first thing he saw, as it had been the last, was Nita's face.

She bent toward him and there were drops of liquid on her cheeks beneath her eyes. Wentworth tried to lift a hand to brush at them, but his hand didn't want to rise. He looked down at it in surprise. No, it wasn't tied. It lifted a very little and the thinness of the fingers struck him as funny. He smiled. He knew the symptoms.

"I see that," he whispered, "police bullets still can't kill me."

Nita dabbed the tears off her cheeks. "Of course they can't, Dick, sweetheart," she said cheerfully. "Bullets just bounce off of you."

Wentworth smiled and the picture faded very far away from him. He dropped into sleep. How many times had bullets pierced him thus and dragged him down to the very brink of death? It was too much of a task for his tired brain. His body was marked by a hundred scars and still his marvelous vitality, the invincible power of his will, could pull him back to life when many another man would have died. Gradually, Wentworth began to realize that the air was balmy and that he was in an automobile camping trailer, stretched out in a lower bunk. He remembered the trailer he had seen parked near Kirkpatrick's home. But how had Nita got away from the policemen? At least one officer had seen the trailer and such a vehicle would be ridiculously easy to trace… He asked Nita that question when his strength came back more fully and saw the color drain from her face. She dropped laxly into a chair.

"You see, Dick," she whispered, "I saw that policeman shoot you and… and I didn't quite know what I was doing after that. I… shot the policeman." Her hands twisted whitely in her lap. "He didn't die, but it was a long time before he was able to tell about the trailer. He hadn't seen much detail and… well, we got away."

Wentworth's thin hand groped out for Nita's and closed tightly about it. She had shot a policeman to save him. It was a violation of the inflexible code which the Spider had established, but… what would he have done if he had seen Nita shot down? He did not need to ask the question. He would have killed, killed! He was curiously apathetic during his recovery, almost dreading to ask the questions he must presently frame about the depredations of the Chief, and the hundreds who must have died meanwhile under the curse of the Dancing Death and the Dissolver. Yet, he could do nothing about it until his strength mended—and things were very pleasant here. He was managing now to creep out into the sun and found himself on a sandy beach in Florida where the warmth was driving the weakness from his body. He and Nita sat side by side through long, subtropical days. They didn't talk much. It was as if both realized that words might shatter the dream in which they were living.

For a dream it was, an interlude between the nightmares that lay behind them and those which would rise again as soon as strength had returned to the Spider's body, Wentworth asked no questions about Nita's reasons for siding with Kirkpatrick as she had. Her case had been stated so fully on that night when she had led him into Horace's trap. In the end, she had been unable to hold to her decision, in the face of the hell that loomed for Dick. The warfare had become too vicious....

Wentworth rolled his head toward her where she lay stretched out beneath a beach umbrella on the sands beside him.

"It just occurred to me to wonder why you were there that night with the trailer," he said, laughing. "Strange that it shouldn't have struck me as curious before. It just seemed too right for you to be there."

Nita looked down at the sand, drew meaningless designs with her fingers. "What were you doing there that night?" she countered.

Wentworth looked back at the ribbed and striped umbrella. "I went there to kidnap Kirkpatrick," he said slowly. "There was no other way to stop all that lying about me, to check his feud against me. I had to stop that or it would be impossible to put an end to the Dancing Death."

NITA LAUGHED, an echo of the bitter mirth that had come so often to the Spider's lips. "You figured things as I did. I went there with the trailer to kidnap Stanley Kirkpatrick also. I had some chloroform… Oh, I didn't think it out in much detail, but with the trailer and drugs I thought I could get him out of the city. After that… I don't know. I thought that if you had a chance, you could straighten things out. I'm sorry…."

Her voice cut off as a man in a coast guardsman's uniform strolled near. He nodded casually and went on past, looking out to sea, but Wentworth's and Nita's eyes followed him. The fact that Nita had escaped from New York with him did not make the Spider any less hunted. His eyes met Nita's. "Strange that they should patrol this beach today, when they never have before," he said slowly.

Nita was on her feet as soon as the man had vanished around a bend of palms. She sped toward the trailer, began throwing their scattered belongings into the car. Wentworth got slowly to his feet, folded the umbrella and moved toward her. He was still terribly weak. The handling of the big umbrella taxed his strength. His lips were very grim as he laboriously helped Nita.

"Leave the trailer," Wentworth told her abruptly. "It only makes it easier to follow us, slows us up. If we only take the car, they may think we're returning."

Nita nodded sharply. "You're right." She threw two suitcases into the rumble seat of the Buick roadster, and five minutes after the coast guard had passed, they pulled out of the place where they had been for three weeks. As they passed a thicket of sago palms, Wentworth caught the movement of several men, but they did not challenge. When he looked back, he saw a uniformed officer striding swiftly toward the trailer they had abandoned. Nita caught sight of him, too, in the rear vision mirror.

"Lucky you wanted to leave the trailer," she whispered. "Oh, Dick, they've found us. They've found us! Why didn't you…."

Wentworth knew the end of the question she would have asked. Why hadn't he permitted the police to consider him dead? Why hadn't he heeded her plea? Wentworth settled back against the cushions staring ahead where the white road and the white sand made a continuous blinding whir before his eyes. He had chosen this harder way because it was necessary for the Spider to come to life and recommence the battle with the new menace. He blew out a slow breath. It was his weakness that made him so reluctant to end their idyll. But it was already ended, wasn't it? That coast guardsman strolling past had finished all their hopes, their peace. He forced his emaciated body more erect in the seat.

"Tell me, Nita," he said quietly.

It was fearful tale that Nita had to tell. The looting of the *Saxon Prince* had been only the first of many such tragedies, nor did the killers always rob after they had loosed their plague of torture. It was as if they killed for the sheer joy of the enterprise, but actually, it was the shrewdest type of terrorism. Whenever the ramshackle cars which the butchers drove appeared, men and women fled in panic. Sometimes machine guns sprayed death into their crowded ranks; sometimes whole batteries of dart-shooting guns and glass bombs of the Dissolver were tossed among the close-packed people.

The Terror had spread beyond the limits of New York, had dipped into Jersey towns, gone westward through Pennsylvania. And everywhere, as soon as the Dancing Death struck, people fled and left their riches to the will of the killers. Sometimes police or banks made a determined fight, but when they did, it was a horrible thing. The defenders were slaughtered, and their tortured bodies left as evidence of what happened to those who stood in the path of the Chief.

In that dark cloud there was only one spot of light, the Spider once more was believed dead. The policeman was sure that his bullets had gone home into the Spider's body and there had been traces... Nita's voice faltered in its clear recital... of blood in the snow. Furthermore, he had not been seen for many weeks. It was true that Corporal Death was operating again....

Wentworth whipped about. *He* was Corporal Death. It was his own creation, a somber faced man who killed terribly with a knife and put his Cross upon the faces of the criminals who answered to his swift justice. There had been two men who had fought in his band when he had been forced into the refuge of Corporal Death, two men who had valiantly cast their lot with him against a completely crooked city government....

NITA SHOOK her head, seeming to read his thoughts. "It is not Pat O'Rourke or Len Roberts," she said. "I got in touch with them, knowing you would want to know." While she talked

Nita's eyes never swerved from the road ahead. She was covering ground rapidly.

"There's a bathing beach ahead," Wentworth said abruptly. "Stop there and we'll rent cabins, change into regular clothing from these bathing suits. They make us conspicuous."

Nita obeyed, and ten minutes later, they were racing on again. At the first city of any size, they would abandon the car and either rent another or take a train. Wentworth was aware that Nita had not looked at him since the discussion of the butchery in New York had begun. Her voice, too, lacked life, but she made no further plea to him to abandon his task. The situation now was as it had been before. He was supposed to be dead... Wentworth knew well the torture she suffered and he appreciated her silence though it saddened him. It became increasingly clear to him that they had come to the parting of the ways—they two who loved so deeply. She had made her final great fight for him when she had betrayed him into police hands, a thing that it was still hard for Wentworth to understand. The Spider's murderous pace was no longer hers. It was grim enough for a man—for a woman it became impossible. She had weakened to save the man she loved from death at Kirkpatrick's home and in doing it she had been forced to shoot a policeman, a thing Wentworth had never done until their baseness made them deserve death more richly than any other type of criminal... Wentworth looked down at his thin hands upon his knees.

"I'm very sorry, Nita," he said, humbly as he felt. "God knows you have deserved better than you have received at my hands. But I cannot...."

Nita said sharply, "I haven't asked you not to go back to the fight. It is quite apparent…" She stopped herself. "I will not be bitter. You've made your choice. It's the end for us, Dick. I thought for a while the night that I was going to kidnap Kirkpatrick that I could come back with you. I thought that our love… And then I shot that poor policeman, did it gladly and without hesitation because I thought he had killed you. Oh, don't you see, Dick, what this life does to you and me? I've killed men before this to help your work. It isn't… woman's work. It isn't even human… Oh, Dick, what I've been afraid of so long has happened. The Spider has… killed Richard Wentworth!"

WENTWORTH STILL looked at his hands. His lips felt feverish, his eyes burning. It was true. There wasn't much of Richard Wentworth left in him, this frail body was no more than a naked will, and that determination was the Spider.

"I'm sorry, Nita," he whispered. It was nothing to say, but it was the only thing that could be said. He could not swerve from his fixed way. It was no longer in him. The Spider had killed Richard Wentworth. "Better stop in the next town," he said slowly. "They'll be tracing this car before long. We'll abandon it, get another." It would have to be a second-hand car and a cheap one. Wentworth's funds had almost vanished. Nita had only her fixed income which, with falling dividends, was only barely enough to support her… They left the Buick, bought a serviceable second-hand car and Wentworth counted money with Nita. She had ample funds to get them to New York.

"I'm going to get another gun," Wentworth told her. "You

wait here while I try to find where to get it. If I don't come back in, say, an hour...."

Nita's hands clung to him. "Oh, Dick, do you have to..." She bit the words off, bowed her head against his chest. Wentworth's arms went about her shoulders, strained her close. His eyes looked blankly before him. He bent to her lips and when he turned to go, Nita clung to his arm. "Dick, lover... the way you kissed me...!"

WENTWORTH LAUGHED, patted her hand and strode off. He bumped into a man, muttered an apology and hurried on, turned a corner. He couldn't see with that damned moisture in his eyes, but Nita must not understand that this was good-bye, not until he was well away from her... Good-bye to love, to life, to everything but thankless service. Wentworth wondered a little at himself, but men had ever turned to warfare and honor, the Wentworths always had....

It was night when the plane set Wentworth down at Newark airport and he shivered in the fresh wind from over the meadows. His blood was thin, his body fever-ridden... He rode the transport bus to New York, took a subway train. He had a definite goal and though it was largely guess-work, he was pretty sure that his guess was right. He alighted from the train at One Hundred Eighty-First Street, west, and took a taxi. Five minutes later, he was climbing laboriously up the stairs that led to the apartment of ex-Detective Bill Horace. He sounded the bell briefly and stood with his feverish eyes on the door. He hoped Horace was home....

The footsteps that moved toward the door were heavy and

slow, those of an old or a broken man. When the lock clicked and Wentworth looked into the eyes of Bill Horace… Horace smiled slowly.

"Hello, Spider," he said, "I didn't think they'd killed you." He stepped aside for Wentworth to come in, utterly without surprise, and with little interest. Wentworth went past him into the living room, sank upon a davenport. He looked curiously at the window that gave on the fire escape. Police had chased him along that route not so very long ago. It seemed fantastic…. He was very tired. Bill Horace was standing in front of him.

"Want a drink? There's some rot-gut rye."

Wentworth said, "Thanks," presently Horace came back with two glasses of whisky, two glasses of water. "How," he said. They drank and Wentworth waited for the warmth to spread over him. He put down the two glasses deliberately, looked into Horace's face.

"Bill," he said, "I used to be Corporal Death. You're he now, aren't you?"

Horace smiled crookedly. The man had taken on years in the weeks since his wife had been kidnaped. Wentworth knew what that aging was. Nita had been in the hands of his enemies many times…. The shudder of the strong drink shook him belatedly. He smiled a little, and Horace dropped down on the davenport beside him.

"Yes, I'm Corporal Death," he said. "How did you guess?"

Wentworth had his thin hands on his knees. He moved the fingers slowly. "Just that, a guess," he said. He wondered if police still watched this place, but he decided it didn't matter. If police came, they wouldn't find Corporal Death and the Spider. Horace was talking....

"They've killed Tony," he said dully. "I know that. After you disappeared, I didn't hear any more. Hell... without her, nothing matters. I... like to kill them." His voice ended on a harsh, rising note that was more horrible than a curse. He repeated his final words. *"I like to kill them!"*

Wentworth lifted his hand to Horace's shoulder. "We'll do some killing together, eh, Bill?"

The breaking of the window glass beside the fire escape was a niagara of sound. Wentworth's eyes went to it almost before the sound reached his ears, or so it seemed. There were two Hindus crouched there on the fire escape. He could see the gleam of the lights within on their white garments, on their eyes... and on the implements in their hands. Each of them carried two, a glass bomb that could contain only the Dissolver, and an air pistol that would fire unerringly the darts of the Dancing Death!

CHAPTER 14
FOUR MEN WHO DIE!

WENTWORTH HAD not waited on the evidence of his eyes. Breaking glass could herald only enemies— and his guns were in his hands when he saw the Hindus with their hideous torture weapons. The thunder of the shots beat on the walls, hammered against Wentworth's eardrums. Mingled with the heavy detonations of his forty-five caliber automatics, he made out the lighter crash of a thirty-eight.

Wentworth smiled slightly before he turned to Horace who sat beside him with a police revolver in his right hand.

"We do pretty well together, Bill," he said.

Horace got to his feet, poking out two empty shells which he dropped into his pocket before substituting fresh shells. "Yes, but you think more quickly. You smashed the bomb and the gun… I only thought of killing them."

Wentworth laughed out loud as he stood. "Let's get out of here. You said you'd learned to shoot from the Spider. You certainly have precision of aim. Both of those men were drilled through the forehead."

Horace's weary face relaxed in a slight smile. "You taught me that trick, too. That shot not only kills but paralyzes. Yes, we'd better go. Have you any plans?"

When they were in Horace's light sedan, cruising quietly along the streets, Wentworth told him. It would take a force attack to defeat and end the depredations of the Chief, not by police, but by men who could and would kill on sight, who had been trained to precision of gun-fire as certain as thought… by Wentworth and Bill Horace, by Ram Singh and Jackson. Horace smiled sleepily at the road ahead of him.

"That means Sing Sing first, to free Ram Singh and Jackson, eh?" He whirled the sedan around a corner and sent it northward over the Albany Post Road. He drove steadily, skillfully, without question.

Wentworth, leaning back in his corner of the seat, eyed him thoughtfully. He knew the symptoms. Here was a man who wanted to die—and die quickly. It was that and vengeance which drove him on rather than a desire to serve. Wentworth's lips pressed together and his eyes dropped to his thin hands. He twisted the fingers idly together....

"The plan," he said drily, "is to forge a paper to get us to the warden and then persuade him to release the prisoners. I will disguise our faces. You will be Corporal Death and, for tonight, I shall pretend to be the Spider."

Horace did not reply. He was silent throughout the trip. Even when they stopped in a tourist camp and put on the disguises, he did not speak. His smile grew and he laughed easily at nothing. He expected to die this night, and he was happy in the thought... They pulled up to the gate of Sing Sing and Horace showed the paper which Wentworth had prepared before the meeting, showed a badge that the Spider had also thought of. They were allowed to drive inside the gate. Wentworth was the Spider tonight but as yet he walked without the hunched back and the limp which characterized the shadowy killer of the night. And his cape was drawn close about him like a coat, his black slouch hat sat more jauntily on his head than was the Spider's custom. He cracked a grim joke with Horace as the former detective got heavily from the car and they moved together toward the door of the warden's quarters behind a guard.

HORACE GLANCED at Wentworth out of the corner of his eyes, then glanced toward the guard. Should he be put out of the way? Wentworth shook his head almost imperceptibly. He thanked the guard courteously as he left them at the door of the warden's office. The warden was a grave, elderly man with gray eyes which were surprisingly kind. He glanced up, but did not rise, waited until Horace came to the desk with his order, which was apparently a permit from New York police for him to see a prisoner. He held it out; the warden glanced down at it, and from across the room, Wentworth struck, hurling a blackjack with deadly accuracy. It caught the warden between the eyes, hurled him back in his chair. As he lolled forward across the desk again, Horace caught him so that he would not injure his face. It had been necessary to do this so that he could not press the alarm signals, the button of which was always at his fingertips. Cautiously, Wentworth and Horace carried him from behind his desk and swiftly revived him. And now Wentworth was fully the Spider, eyes gleaming beneath the down-slanting brim of his black hat, hunched back giving him a sinister appearance to match his reputation... The warden came back to consciousness and his face reddened with a hard anger. Wentworth smiled down on him.

"I'm afraid," he said gently, "that you did not recognize me when I came in. I trust that you do now?"

The warden lifted his gray eyes, that were cold as ice now and his lips tightened. "Yes, I know you. I had thought you dead. You were here once before, in the death house."

Wentworth shook his head. "That is why I am here tonight, because people choose to confuse me with Wentworth, who is a much inferior man. Good, I grant you, but still inferior. Two men of his are in cells here for helping Wentworth to escape a false arrest. I don't consider that exactly just, so I'll have to ask you to free them. It should have been attended to long ago, but unfortunately…" Wentworth shrugged. "I have been occupied elsewhere."

The warden laughed grimly. "Nothing doing."

Wentworth smiled apologetically. "I rather expected you to refuse." He took a small black case from his pocket, extracted a hypodermic needle. The warden looked at it and could not keep the color from draining out of his cheeks, but he asked no questions, merely sat tight-lipped and defiant. "Just a bit of *morphia.*" Wentworth told him pleasantly. "Your heart is quite sound? Yes, I thought so." He made the injection in the throat with a swift ease that defeated the warden's intention of battle, despite the revolver Horace held on his head. In moments, he sagged unconscious in his chair. And then Horace saw one of the Spider's really great impersonations. He swiftly donned the warden's clothing, then sat before a mirror with a strong light on his face, removed materials that he had previously prepared from pockets of his cape. It was swift and efficient work. When it was finished, the warden sat in a dark corner in Wentworth's clothing, Horace seated beside him. Wentworth took his place behind the desk, after looking over the prison records, pressed a button. A guard stepped in and saluted.

"Bring 23495 and 23496 here," he ordered curtly. His tone and manner were perfect. The guard saluted again and Wentworth began to talk casually to Horace, still using the warden's tone, perfecting himself in it. "There can be no doubt," he said, "that these two prisoners were closely associated with the man, Wentworth. Whether he is the Spider I can't say, but these two…."

He kept it up, slowly, gravely, until the two prisoners were brought in. Ram Singh had been allowed to retain his full beard, but he had no turban. Still, his bearing and that of Jackson was proud and soldierly. Their eyes met those of Wentworth directly and without quailing.

"**BRING THEIR** clothing," Wentworth told the guard shortly. He turned to Horace. "I still think it is extremely dangerous to take these two prisoners to New York, despite what the Grand Jury thinks. You are two men…" The door closed behind the guard, but Wentworth did not relax his warden manner. He spoke sternly to Ram Singh and Jackson, though his heart leaped at the sight of their well-loved faces again. He longed to seize their hands in welcome… "You have been called before the Grand Jury in New York to testify concerning your master, Richard Wentworth, who is accused of being the Spider," he said. "I need not inform you that if you tell the whole truth, it will make it much easier for you here. There might even be a parole. I must warn you also that no attempt to escape—" here the guard came in with two bundles of clothing—"can possibly succeed and that the penalties in case of any attempt will be the maximum that it is in my power to inflict. You understand me, prisoners?"

Jackson's jaw was hard set. Ram Singh's dark eyes flashed hostilely. It was Jackson who spoke. "You may as well save yourself the trouble," he said flatly, "We don't know anything and if we did, we wouldn't tell."

"You will get nowhere with that attitude, my man," Wentworth told him sternly. "We have been lenient with you here, but…" The guard was gone, his footsteps receding down the hall. Wentworth got up from behind the desk, walked up until he stood directly in front of Jackson. "Get into your clothes, Sergeant," he said, in his natural voice, "and let's get the hell out of here."

An incredulous joy leaped into Jackson's face. Ram Singh pivoted with a cry barely choked in his throat. *"Sahib!"* he muttered brokenly. He dropped to his knee and snatched Wentworth's hand to his lips, but Wentworth would not have it. He drew the Sikh to his feet, embraced him. "My brother," he called him. Jackson wrung his hand until their fingers were numb, then with the impetuosity of his Gascon forbears, threw his arms about Wentworth's shoulders, pounding his back.

"God, sir," he whispered, "we were sure you were dead. Sure of it. We…."

Horace was on his feet. "We'd best be hurrying. The warden is coming out of it a little, I think."

"Corporal Death," Wentworth introduced him. "Now, hurry, you two, into those clothes. You'll go out handcuffed to us, of course. Keep your faces sullen and resentful. You're being taken to testify against a friend, you know. All the guards out there will know that by now…."

Swiftly as they dressed, Wentworth was back into his own clothing even more quickly. As they went out the door, he checked a moment and called back. "Thank you, Warden. We'll have them back by Friday, I think."

The warden's voice apparently answered, "Good night, gentlemen. Remember, prisoners, your future welfare depends upon your conduct." It was not ventriloquism, but Wentworth speaking in an altered voice, his lips invisible to the guards. He closed the door, yanked sharply on the handcuff that bound Ram Singh's right wrist to his left and followed Horace down the hall. The warden was in his desk chair, the light focused away from his face. He was beginning to come out of the morphia, of which he had been given a light dose, but it would be a half hour before he had sufficient control of his faculties to start a pursuit... Ten minutes after leaving the warden's office, they left the prison gate and sped back along the road to New York City. Five minutes afterward, they turned off the main highway and sought the back country routes. It would take them longer to reach the city, but here they were less liable to pursuit....

JACKSON RELIEVED Horace at the wheel. He was happiest when driving or flying a plane and he sang soldier songs as he bowled them along. His happiness overflowed. When he ceased, Ram Singh's harsh nasal voice went on, a chant of his warlike people, the song of the Singhs, the lions of the Sikhs. He improvised and worked in the glory of his master, the killer, the brave fighter. He sang in his native tongue, Punjabi... Wentworth had given the two of them only one message: "We go to fight, probably to die. The end is near for all of us." Even Horace looked happier after that. He turned to Wentworth on the back seat....

"Do you have any plan of action now?" the ex-detective asked.

Wentworth permitted himself to smile. It was a grim expression. "Just one. To find the Chief and his hideout, to kill the last man of them. I still have no idea of the identity of the Chief. Two of the leaders I have met—or three—the doctor who contrived these torture weapons, a woman called Tarsa, and a Spaniard named Pascual Madrigas. I think the man is the Chief, but I am far from certain. I have killed two men who wore the black robe and hood supposed to be the clothes of the Chief and both of them were Hindus...."

"Wah!" Ram Singh interrupted. "There is one, *sahib*, on whom thy servant claims the privilege of wreaking the vengeance of all the Sikhs. A vile Thug who calls himself Raj Singh! *Wah!* Never did the order of the lions recognize such as him!"

Wentworth laughed softly. "He is thine, my warrior. He has called himself my servant."

Ram Singh laughed, too, and the sound was warlike as a battle cry. "Then, my master, thou soon shalt lose a servant."

Horace listened to the talk quietly. Hindustani, of course, he could not understand though no one could mistake the fierce exultation of Ram Singh's tone. "I think," said Horace, "that I may have a clue to the Chief. I managed to make a prisoner talk before he died and he told of a raid planned for tomorrow that was to make them all rich. Kali would feast, he said, and he mentioned Washington. Tomorrow is the day. There is no plan to seize the government, but I understood that the Chief would terrorize the entire capital and then hold important officials for ransom. Perhaps, even the President...."

Wentworth nodded his head. He could well believe such daring tactics of the men who had spread slaughter like a red paint over the eastern half of the country. "You have no clue as to the time of the day they will strike, or where they are hiding now?"

Horace shook his head. "I will guarantee that they aren't in New York any longer. That's all I know."

Wentworth nodded slowly. "The best way to travel to Washington will be to seize a plane. We'll have to take the pilot with us to prevent an alarm before we're ready. Jackson, you know this section pretty thoroughly."

Jackson said, "Yes, Major."

Wentworth leaned back at his ease though his brain raced ahead with terrible clarity. The battle tomorrow in Washington would be the climax of all the Chiefs efforts. If it succeeded, there was little chance that he could be stopped soon, for his strength would be too great. He would have all the allies he wished, untold wealth. Tomorrow he must be stopped, or it would be too late.

Confidence sat upon Wentworth's shoulders like a rich mantle. He would win, he felt, because it would be the Spider's last battle. His strength and spirit were drained and his heart was leaden. It would be his last fight because Wentworth did not expect to survive it. It was not that the Spider would ever throw his life away as long as he felt his country needed it, but he knew that the essential fire that had driven him through so many fierce and bloody fights had died down; he would not go into this fight joyfully as of old, but driven by duty with a grim necessity to kill. He felt that it would not serve. It was, truly, the end.

CHAPTER 15
A LIFE FOR A LIFE!

THE SEIZURE of the plane was carried off without difficulty and the pilot finally agreed to cooperate with them when he found out on what perilous mission the four were speeding. Wentworth discarded the disguise of the Spider and resumed his own identity.

"The Spider himself might be there," he explained to Horace. "I have a notion he would object to anyone else appearing in his role."

Horace and the pilot looked at him curiously. Wentworth's persistence in denying by implication that he was the Spider had a curious effect upon the former detective. He wasn't convinced and yet reiteration was wearing on his disbelief. He shook his head at Wentworth's statement and Wentworth shrugged, went forward to where Jackson sat at the controls. His presence was not needed, but he wanted to be alone. He could not afford to tell them his real reason for discarding the Spider. His premonition of disaster and death had grown on him through the long and tiresome night. When he died, it would be gloriously fighting... under his own name. His ominous thoughts did not dampen his courage, rather they would inspire him to new miracles of strength. He must find and slay the Chief before he fell....

The late winter dawn greeted them at Washington and for hours, their vigilance brought them no reward. They slept in relays at the hotel they had chosen while the other members of the party kept watch over the residence of the one man whom

Two Mongols bound Tony's arms.

The Sikh took his place at the levers.

Horace knew definitely to be threatened, the Secretary of the Treasury, Branch Hopkins. He was confined to his bed with a severe cold, but it was probable that would only make it easier for the men of the Chief.

Wentworth himself had chosen the hour when he thought it most likely the blow would come: the crowded, noon-time luncheon hour when the streets would be filled with potential victims for the slaughterers, when terror and panic would spread most quickly. Wentworth kept his watch inconspicuously. He had on a chauffeur's cap and he sat behind the wheel of a rented car which he had parked nearby. It was unlike him to be nervous over approaching battle, but he was aware of a mounting tension in his breast. It brought a smile to his lips, but his hands strayed often to the guns beneath his arms. It was a reflex, a need of reassurance....

When the break came, it was without any warning at all, on the heels of slaughter and death. One of those battered automobiles which New York had learned to flee as if it bore the plague in its exhaust gases turned into G Street, NW, on which Hopkins had his home. It was two blocks from Wentworth, but even so, he spotted it immediately, and his hand went to the door latch, then to his guns. He was not sure, yet, but....

The alarm came with a blast of machine-gun fire. Two Thompsons were speaking from the slowly moving automobile, one directed to each side of the street. It was pitiless, incredibly wanton—a wholesale blast of lead into crowds of men and women who sauntered forth to lunch of were returning leisurely to resume the afternoon's toil. Into their midst, stalked Death.

SLAVES OF THE MURDER SYNDICATE

Forty-five caliber slugs, striking even more viciously because of the lengthened barrel from which they sped, hammered men and women to the pavement, smashed sunny life into the blackness of death. The car was still two blocks away. Before Wentworth could get his car under way, they would be within range, so he stepped clear of the limousine, crouched behind it and drew his automatic. Damnable to have to wait for the killers while more people died by the second. The killers were still too far away to see enough—to stop them. Their bullets swept the sidewalks clean, spilled crumpled and distorted piles of human beings upon the pavements, filled the air with a cacophony of pain and terror, shrieks of women and hoarse, formless shouts of men dying in agony....

A POLICE officer sprang to the middle of the street throwing down with his revolver. Before he squeezed the trigger, he was wrapped in flaming lead. The bullets bent him double, hammered him backward, rolling, continued to claw and jerk at his body while the arms and legs threshed in death agony. A woman stalled a car she was driving, flopped from the driver's seat and tried to run. She snatched her skirts up in her hands and teetered crazily on high heels. The machine gunner cut her legs from under her and left her lying there, screaming, trying to drag herself along on stiff and useless forearms.

It was terribly hard to wait there behind the auto for the killers to come to him, but these things were happening in split fractions of seconds and the fate of the policeman showed only too plainly what would happen to a man who dared to attack in the open... The chatter of the machine gun ceased as abruptly as it had started. Missiles of terror still sped from the car though Wentworth could no longer hear the sound of their discharge. A woman, running in the rear of the fleeing mob, ceased to retreat and whirled to face the killers. She stood like that through a half dozen hard heartbeats, then she screamed and began the dervish whirl of the Dancing Death. She spun and hopped with a horrid grace as if she were the *premiere danseuse* in a macabre ballet. She soon had a chorus of a dozen men and women to keep her mortal company. Others ran crazily in circles before their legs collapsed and the Dissolver began to melt their limbs from their bodies....

Now, at last, the automobile came within the extreme limit of Wentworth's range. He waited for seconds longer while the fearful carnage continued. Their Thompsons would have the range of him, or rather accuracy at longer range. He could not risk a premature shot, but... Wentworth's lips were drawn back now from his teeth as finally he lined on the head of the death-car's driver. His finger caressed the trigger... and the driver died. The car spun in a tight circle to the left, rammed a stalled automobile and stopped dead. The killers ceased their torture murders and gripped machine guns, hunting for the man who had struck at them. Carefully, Wentworth lined up again. There were three men in the car. He fired once, twice, before the remaining man found him and he had time to get his Thompson in action. He squeezed the trigger and swept along the curbing, lifted to drill the auto shield behind which Wentworth crouched... and died with a bullet through his forehead.

It was not until then that Wentworth realized a second car

had been working up the street from the opposite direction. They had seen the fate of their companions and instead of rushing to the attack, they turned and fled, spreading death as they raced away. Wentworth hesitated between pursuit and the need to keep watch over Hopkins' home. It was not that the preservation of the Secretary of the Treasurer was more important than pursuit, but Wentworth thought that some leaders might come for Hopkins and it was the leaders whom the Spider longed to meet. If he slaughtered a hundred of these minor butchers, he would only wound, not kill, the conspiracy.

He straightened, rapidly reloading his weapons, heard a crisp, advancing footstep behind him and tried to whirl. He got half about, had a brief glimpse of glittering black eyes which were ablaze with hatred and a blast of light blinded him, light that was a crashing blow upon his head… The leaders had arrived—and the Spider was out of the fight!

HIS AWAKENING was far from the silken ease of his previous recovery in the power of the Chief of the Dancing Death. His arms were bound painfully behind him. His legs were fastened immovably to some object he could not see in the darkness. The pain in his head was intolerable, but he forced himself to move it vigorously until increasing circulation lightened its misery. Then be pronounced names into the darkness:

"Horace? Ram Singh? Jackson?"

It was Jackson who answered, his voice bitter with mockery. "All present and accounted for, Major. They got us, every damned one, along with about everybody of importance in Washington. I understand that Commissioner Kirkpatrick was on a visit to the Department of Justice and was taken prisoner along with the rest. Quite a neat haul."

"Thank you, Jackson," Wentworth said dully. He lay staring with wide open eyes into the darkness. The criminals had everything their way, now, with the heads of the government in their hands. Even Kirkpatrick had fallen prey. There was no use in speculating on his own and his followers' fate. They would be killed as painfully as possible as an example to the prisoners held for ransom, perhaps as a demonstration to the emissaries of the ransom payers… Wentworth could tell by the numb cramping of his limbs that he had been bound for a long time….

A door opened abruptly, brilliant white light from the ceiling blinded Wentworth for a while and when he could see again, Tarsa stood over him. She wore no harem charmer's garb tonight, but she was cloaked from shoulders to ankle in a robe of heavy yellow silk which draped exquisitely to the rounded lines of her body.

"So sorry, Spider," she murmured, "that I couldn't grant you a private audience this time. I'll concede the pleasure of our last meeting, but you'll agree that it was rather costly to the Chief…."

Wentworth glanced beyond her. These were no Hindus who stood ready to help her, but burly men from the north of China, stripped naked to the waist as befitted torturers, which Wentworth had no doubt they were. Each one wore a long, slim knife in a sheath at his waist. If he could only get his hands on one of those blades… Tarsa bent low beside Wentworth, her long green eyes speculatively on his.

"I wish that you had not been such a fool," she said. She cut

Wentworth's bonds. He was too wise to attempt any action with his numbed legs and arms. He could scarcely stand and two of the heavily muscled men seized him by either arm and led him, with dragging feet, from the room.

Along a white hall that was vaguely reminiscent of a hospital corridor, Wentworth was led and soon he heard the echoes of other feet behind him. He was not going alone to his fate… Wentworth was past thought, though hope had not deserted him. It would be impossible for him to do anything until control returned to his limbs. What action he would take would depend on his situation at that time….

DOUBLE SLIDING doors opened and Wentworth was wheeled roughly through them and into a large, white room built like an amphitheatric operating room except that no antiseptic glass separated the spectators' seats from the arena. Instead of an operating table, in the middle of the room there stood a huge machine like a flat-bed press. The slotted metal table was arranged so that it would slide beneath a cylinder as large as a steam-rollers drum. The cylinder bristled with long, iron spikes which would fit neatly into the slots that were in the surface of the table….

Wentworth's eyes went curiously over the seats of the amphitheater. They were packed with men, and among their ranks were a score of well-known faces. There was Secretary of the Treasury Hopkins, Edgar Francis, chief of the Bureau of Investigation, and the Secretary of State. There was Stanley Kirkpatrick in a front seat just across the arena from Wentworth. When their eyes met, both men smiled… Each of those prisoners was handcuffed to his seat and in the aisle stood more of the bare-chested Mongols, each with a slim knife and a long-lashed whip....

The Chiefs supply of man power seemed to be without end... Wentworth tried to see some way out of his dilemma, but apparently there was none. The two powerful Mongols kept tight hold on his wrists. Even if he escaped them, there were dozens of others standing nearby. All these captives would be helpless to lend assistance. Yet what hope was there for America, for Wentworth's people, if he failed to smash his way clear? Here all the dignitaries of the nation were held for ransom and there was that incredible machine which must be a new torture device....

The other prisoners had arrived on the scene and were posted at wide intervals about the machine, which, obviously, was to be the center of interest. Wentworth was opposite the roller on one side, Ram Singh on the other. Horace and Jackson were on opposite sides of the arena nearer the end of the table. Their faces were grim, but as hopeless as were Wentworth's own thoughts. This thing that was happening was inconceivable. It was a dream conjured out of that blow upon the head... Abrupt silence fell upon the entire chamber and Wentworth turned to see a triumphal procession entering through the double doors. First came Tarsa, followed by Señor Madrigas, and their damnable Doctor, all in long yellow robes, and behind them walked circumspectly a man whose head was covered in a black hood and whose eyes stared out through slits, as black and hostile as those of a serpent. The Chief!

Wentworth frowned at his approach. He was dubious. Twice, he had slain men in the black robes of the Chief and each time he had killed only an underling. Might this not also be an imposture, another hireling of Tarsa and Madrigas masquerading to foil their enemies? The leaders stood aside and Wentworth saw what had been hidden behind them. The Bearded Sikh who had been so terrible a servant to the Chief throughout his mad butchery, appeared in the doorway, carrying the almost naked body of a struggling woman. A yellow, silken robe was about her, but her fighting… A gasp that was at once torture and delight rose from a man's throat. Bill Horace struggled violently against the men who gripped his arms.

"Tony!" he shouted. "Tony!"

THE GIRL ceased her struggling in the arms of the powerful Hindu and turned her pale face toward the man who shouted. She stretched out her arms. Wentworth's teeth locked together fiercely. Bill Horace had thought his wife dead. Doubtless now he wished that she were! God, what a terrible reunion for man and wife. Tarsa spoke to the Sikh and incredibly, he set the girl upon the floor. She ran to Horace, threw her arms about his neck, buried her blonde head upon his chest. He could not embrace her for Mongols still gripped his wrists in an unshakable grasp. Only a moment was Tony allowed to cling to her husband, then the full cruelty of the thing that Tarsa had done became apparent. The Sikh snatched Tony from Horace's neck, lifted her bodily and laid her flat on her back on the table of the torture machine.

In a trice, two Mongols had leaped forward, bound her arms to the steel plate, then all stepped back and the Sikh, moving with the slow majesty of which all his race were capable, circled

171

to a great lever that jutted from the side of the machine. He was within two yards of the captive Ram Singh and a stream of harsh Punjabi poured from Ram Singh's throat. The other Sikh flinched, whirled and struck Ram Singh heavily across the face, after which he returned to the lever. Wentworth had for a moment strained at the hands that held him, but he knew the uselessness of it and relaxed. He must not prepare them for the break he would presently make....

His involuntary struggle had come at the moment when, with sick agony, he realized the use to which the devilish machine was to be put. Tony was stretched out helplessly on the table, her eyes moving ceaselessly from the huge roller with its spikes back to where Bill Horace struggled frantically with his captors. The Sikh had his hand on the long lever. It was obvious that when he moved it, the heavy cylinder with its dagger-like spikes would roll over the fair body of Tony Horace. What would be left would be scarcely human....

The men in the seats were mad with the horror of what they knew was to come. They shouted and fought the steel shackles that held them, all save one. Stanley Kirkpatrick sat with his face like iron, working on the lock of the handcuff that pinioned his right arm. The Mongols stalked up and down the aisles, lashing out with their long whips. Slowly, silence fell again over the amphitheater... It was then that Tarsa spoke and Wentworth's eyes turned narrowly to her. Was it possible that this woman whom twice he had held it in his power to kill, was the real leader of this monster conspiracy? He looked at her pale, smiling mouth, at the cruelty of her long green eyes and still he doubted. How could a woman rule these men of the East…?

"I see, my friends," came the caressing voice of Tarsa, "that you have already guessed the purpose of my little machine. It has been used before this—to reward unfaithful servants…."

Great dry sobs were shaking Bill Horace's body. He still struggled, but there was no slightest chance that he would be able to break from the two Mongols, one of whom had pressed the point of his knife against the ex-detective's throat.

"Demonstrate, Raj Singh," said Tarsa.

The giant Sikh, striped to his turban and a loin cloth, leaned his weight against the long lever. The table began to move very slowly toward the revolving cylinder of spikes. Tony's teeth clenched on her lips until the blood ran. Men shuddered and tried to hide their eyes….

Horace fought to fling himself to his knees. "In God's name," he pleaded hoarsely. "Kill me in her place, you fiend!"

Tarsa smiled and nodded her head and the Sikh moved the lever in reverse. The rumbling of the machine stopped. Horace's face lighted with joy.

"Bless you," he cried. "Oh bless you!" He bowed his head and the tears rolled down his cheeks. It was Tony who was pleading now. Let her be the one to die….

Tarsa laughed trillingly. In any other place, men might have thrilled to the beauty of her laughter, but coming in this scene of death and insupportable grief, it was a rasp on raw nerves.

"My friends," she called again. "Your representatives are here to arrange for your ransom. I have told them that the death they see here tonight is what will lie in store for you, if the ransom is not forthcoming. Every night I shall feed one of you to the machine here until the last ransom is paid. I had intended to use this useless woman as the first example, but their love moves me to pity. I have an alternative to propose...."

Not even Bill Horace was any longer deceived as to her mercy. The mockery in her tones, the very way in which she pronounced the word "pity" struck chill horror to the heart. Tarsa sensed that and laughed again, and this time the cruelty that could curve her pale lips and light those long green eyes was in the sound.

"Yes, yes, an alternative," she said. She clapped her hands and Horace was brought forward, carried to a place beside the machine. Tony rolled her head toward him, tried to smile with her bitten lips. "It doesn't matter, Bill," she whispered, "now that I've seen you again."

Wentworth had watched and listened with agony tugging at his heart. What good were all his efforts if they ended in misery and pain such as this for those who served with him? His was the fault that Tony lay now upon that steel altar of bloody sacrifice, that Bill Horace's face was twisted with horror which would never again leave his eyes however much he tried bravely to smile.

Wentworth glanced stealthily and secretly about. Kirkpatrick was working on the handcuff with the sweat beading his forehead. Abruptly a Mongol reached out with the long-lashed whip, struck again and again across Kirkpatrick's broad shoulders. The commissioner bit his lips in agony, and even that frail hope was gone. Wentworth fought to keep his muscles lax until the crucial moment. The Mongols beside him were grinning, licking their lips in anticipation....

"My alternative," murmured Tarsa and the room was breathless to hear her. "My alternative is a little matter of tossing a bomb of my favorite chemical, the Dissolver." She paused and looked about her until her eyes reached Wentworth and her long lips smiled. "Do you think, my dear Spider, that your clothing is impervious to the Dissolver?"

As the full import of what the woman proposed struck the prisoners, a gasp went up. She proposed that Bill Horace to save his wife from this steel mangler, kill the man he revered above all others by means of the most potent and fearful of her weapons—the salt that dissolved human flesh!

Wentworth threw back his head and sent his laughter racketing against the ceiling, at the skylight which gave on the night sky. It was madness, that laughter, and it was madness that narrowed Wentworth's eyes. It wasn't credible, but up there, thirty feet above the heads of the torturers, he thought he had seen a white face staring down through the glass. The sight almost stopped his laughter. He broke it off, bowed as well as he could with the grip of the Mongols on his arms.

"I'll be glad to be of service to my friend, Bill Horace," he said. "Long life and happiness, Tony."

CHAPTER 16
ENTER THE SPIDER!

WENTWORTH DID not glance toward Tarsa as he spoke, but looked deep into the eyes of Bill Horace. Even Tony's eyes turned to him. In their life, the Spider was a more personal element than to these others. He had saved Bill's life more than once in those olden times and it was he who had engineered Bill's promotion to detective which had permitted them to marry. Perhaps something of that was in their minds as they tried to meet his careless smile. It was only a moment that their eyes met, then Wentworth turned to the leaders.

"I won't argue about the fact that you are going to kill me," he said pleasantly. "A man has to die some time… But I want to disabuse your mind of one thing. I am Richard Wentworth. If you think I am the Spider, you will probably discover your error very painfully some day. Tell me, though, before this execution takes place, what security do you offer Bill Horace and Tony if Bill obeys your orders?"

Wentworth spoke with a calm steadiness, a distinctness of enunciation that drew his words out interminably. It was an old trick of his, to stall for time when no opening for his wits offered itself, hoping against hope that something might develop while he talked. His mind was toying with the memory of that pale face seen through the skylight. He could not be mistaken about having seen it, but perhaps it was only some guard posted up there to insure the safety of these killers….

Tarsa shrugged. "I offer them no security. They must die, but if Horace does as I wish they can die together and painlessly. Otherwise, I shall reverse his wife's position upon the table and drag her, very slowly, feet first, beneath the roller. I am quite sure it won't kill her until her legs and pelvis have been crushed, probably not until her ribs collapse and compress the lungs. If she faints, we will stop the roller until she has been revived." The woman was rolling the words on her tongue. It was plain that she had some especial reason to hate Tony Horace....

"You must agree, Bill," Wentworth said calmly. "We won't ask Tony to suffer that torture...."

Tarsa lifted her hand, and one of the Mongols strode from the hall, came back swiftly with a small, glass bomb. Another man set a metal screen behind and on both sides of Horace so that he could only hurl the bomb at Wentworth.

"Remember, Horace," Tarsa said calmly. "If there is any mistake in your aim, your wife will pay for it, and you will suffer the same penalty. Raj...."

The grinding of the machine started again, a Mongol gingerly handed Horace the bomb. He stood with his teeth clenched on his lip, his eyes in agony upon Tony's face. She was smiling bravely as the table slid slowly toward the advancing roller....

"Don't throw, Bill," she whispered. "I will soon be dead and the Spider has done us no harm that we should destroy him..." Her voice broke.

Bill Horace looked from her to the bomb in his hand, looked into Wentworth's face. Very slowly, Wentworth winked at him, then rolled his eyes upward. He lifted his face with his eyes closed as if in prayer, but through his half-lowered lids he saw something that brought joy throbbing through him with a fierceness he could scarcely contain. If only Bill had understood and would delay his throw for a few seconds....

THE CRASH of the automatic was deafening, coming as it did from over the heads of the assembled men and torturers. For a moment, they did not know the direction from which the gun had spoken, only saw the figure of the hooded man collapse forward to the floor with a slowness that told of death striking swiftly through his body. Bill Horace had seen Wentworth's upward glance and, with the shot, he stared upward. A shout of joy rose in his throat. With a lunge, he hurled the metal screen on his right to the floor, whipped back his arm and hurled the Dissolver bomb straight at Tarsa!

She was pointing an automatic upward, but even her supreme courage was not proof against the terror of that hurtling torture bomb. She ducked aside and the bomb went past her, struck the chest of the fiendish scientist who had invented it, splashed on him and Madrigas. Wentworth was still held motionless against the low barricade about the arena.

"Look! Look!" he shouted at the Mongols who gripped him. The men stared toward the skylight and Wentworth seized his opportunity. He kicked the man on his right in the groin, threw all his weight into a heave on the wrist of the other Mongol. The man was pulled violently off-balance and Wentworth's hand darted to his throat.

The entire chamber was in a mad turmoil, prisoners shouting their fears and hopes to the ceiling. Gradually, one cry thrust through all the others, became a triumphant chant. "The Spider! The Spider comes!"

There could be no mistaking that ominous, caped figure slowly swinging down from the opened skylight upon a slender silken line that could be nothing other than the famous "web" which had figured in so many of the Spider's exploits. There was a gun in each hand of the descending figure and they hammered, hammered out death in a swift rhythm of destruction. There was one danger that the Spider seemed to ignore—Tarsa had thrown herself to the floor and, from beneath the body of a slain Mongol, she leveled her gun upward. Wentworth could not see Tarsa's body, but her gun hand, pointing rigidly toward the dangling figure, was all too fearfully plain.

Wentworth's brain was reeling with the apparition that came down like a bolt from the blue to save them at the last heart-beat of life. He could not fathom this quick answer to his direful prophecy, made to Tarsa more in hope of delaying the fatal moment that was to come than with any especial desire to deny the fact of his double identity. But it must be a friend, and a friend who had arrived in the nick of time. He must turn that ready gun! Yet Tarsa was twenty feet away, too far for a leap to put him there in time to help. Wentworth knew these things without calculation, as a man who has fought many times with a sword parries without thought. He stooped to the body of the unconscious Mongol at his feet, snatched the knife from his belt and threw it in one continuous flow of movement. The sliver of bright steel flew like an arrow across the chamber, transfixed that threatening wrist the instant the finger closed on the trigger. The recoil whipped the weapon from the nerveless hand, but there was a faint cry from the dangling figure that was almost to the floor at long last. The false Spider could fire no longer, but that did not delay the attack. Throwing off the rope by which the descent had been made, the sinister figure in black leaped toward the steel table which was dragging Tony Horace to her death….

Wentworth saw now what the flurry of swift action had hidden from him before. Horace was nowhere to be seen. Undoubtedly, he had been felled by one of the Mongols, striking from behind, and the woman was dangerously close to the steel claws of the roller. Tony was screaming, screaming, rolling her blonde head in awful dread. The bearded Sikh, Wentworth saw, was leaning hard on the lever, lips dragged back from his teeth. As the false Spider leaped to the attack, three of the half naked Mongols leaped forward with flashing knives, and there was nothing but an empty gun to oppose them!

With despair in his heart, Wentworth hurled himself toward the gun Tarsa had dropped, but the intervention came from a source that Wentworth had not expected. Straight from the skylight, thirty feet above, plunged a dark figure. No rope supported that diving fury. Feet first into the middle of the mêlée, the figure lanced and two Mongols went down under the blow of his feet, never to arise. With a shout of acclaim, Wentworth hailed the new arrival. It was Eddie Blackmon!

There was no time to speculate on the strange arrival of the man who twice had tried to kill the Spider, yet who was now so obviously launching himself into the battle on the side of the Spider. Wentworth had the gun finally. He sprang with his back to the wall and slowly, coolly, began to shoot. He picked his men with care, always dropping the Mongol who most threatened some one. His bullets had freed Jackson, and the sturdy Gascon was dashing into the battle beside the machine. One of Tony Horace's hands had been slashed free and she pulled her yellow head away from the roller in the nick of time.

Slowly, Wentworth straightened from against the wall. He had two bullets left, but the Mongols had fled. Ram Singh, knife in hand, was circling about the false Sikh, who opposed his steel with steel. But Wentworth's interference would not be welcome there.

Wentworth walked heavily toward the caped figure beside the machine. The imitation of the Spider was perfect. There was the same hunched shoulders, the grim, long nosed face with its bitter mouth.

"Spider," said Wentworth, "You have saved the day again."

Kirkpatrick's shout from his seat across the arena was filled with unutterable terror, with a fierce haste. "Watch out, Spider. The woman. A bomb...."

Wentworth snatched at the hands of the false Spider and tried to spin aside from the path of the bomb Kirkpatrick warned them of. It could only be Tarsa, and Wentworth remembered for the first time that he had not killed the woman, only pierced her wrist. As he tried to snatch their savior from danger, he twisted about and saw that he would be too late. Regardless of what he did, that bomb laden with the fearful Dissolver for which there was no antidote would smash over him and the false Spider. Tarsa's arm was already flashing forward, her face twisted with a deforming hate....

There was a touch of the eternal cosmic justice which the gods sometimes decree in what happened then. The man whose wife had been murdered by these fiends in search of a "volunteer" to test their fearful weapons leaped forward to the woman who, Wentworth now realized, must be the leader of this fiendish group of criminals. Eddie Blackmon caught the hand that held the Dissolver bomb, threw his other arm about Tarsa's waist and lifted her off her feet. Whether it was the impact of stopping that throw or whether Blackmon's hand closed too tightly over Tarsa's, there was no way of telling, but screams revealed that the bomb had broken, the screams of Tarsa!

Blackmon's face was twisted with the pain that gripped him, but he did not check his movements. He continued to lift Tarsa until her Dissolver-tortured body was high above his head, then he hurled her violently from him toward the torture machine which had almost taken the life of Bill Horace's wife. Tarsa's scream rose to a higher, an incredible pitch. She struck against the spiked roller.

Blackmon, his face distorted, his right arm melting away into nothingness before the assault of the Dissolver, stooped to the floor and caught up a knife. With his left hand, he drove the blade up to its hilt in his chest. For a moment, he wavered on his feet. Then agony blotted from his face and his lips smiled a little before he sank down upon the floor amid the bodies of men on whom he wreaked vengeance.

Wentworth saw these things, as he raced forward, and as he

ran, Ram Singh pressed the false Sikh backward toward the machine. He slipped through the other's guard, struck deeply with his knife. It was the end. With his teeth showing through his beard, Ram Singh picked up the wounded Hindu and tossed him bodily to the torture table.

"Stop the machine!" Wentworth cried.

He was already too late. The body of the woman who had brought this evil to the nation revolved downward on the roller to meet the moving body of the Hindu who had enacted her direful plots and the two of them went together between the cruel steels that they had built to murder others. There was a gasp, a faint moan and Wentworth saw that the fake Spider had fallen to the floor. In a leap, he reached the masked figure, caught it up in his arms. He looked into Kirkpatrick's eyes across the arena.

"Commissioner Kirkpatrick, and you others," he said. "I call you others to witness that this man who calls himself the Spider saved our lives. But there is a heavy price on his head as there is on mine. He is wounded. I am carrying him to safety and you can prosecute me for it, if you wish."

Kirkpatrick's stern face smiled slowly. "Dick," he said. "I ask your forgiveness and Nita's for the things that have been done. I accused you falsely in a dozen instances, but I thought it was for your own good, to end a life which, the evidence of my eyes now proves—" his voice was ironic with doubt, with his disbelief of the thing he saw—"could not be possible. I see you and the Spider simultaneously; therefore you are not the Spider.

The thing that you do now, in saving the Spider, is beyond my jurisdiction. I doubt that anyone will prosecute."

Wentworth was already moving toward the double doors leading from the fearful arena of death. He saw Tony Horace helping Bill to his feet, saw Ram Singh striding exultantly after him.

"Free Kirkpatrick and the others, Jackson," Wentworth called. "Ram Singh, you and Jackson will surrender yourselves at once to Commissioner Kirkpatrick." They could not be held, except for the prison break, and Wentworth knew they would be pardoned when it was proved they were not guilty of the crime charged, helping a criminal to escape the law. For Wentworth, thanks to the figure he carried in his arms, was no longer a criminal in the eyes of the law. He would be restored to his properties, to his old life of wealth which he need leave only to fight the battles of the people. The last menace had gone from the earth when Tarsa had died between those rollers....

Wentworth's face should have been joyful, but it was grave with anxiety. He stumbled as he walked with that burden in his arms. He almost ran, and his heart throbbed with desperate fear, with straining hope... Once outside the double doors, he whipped the mask from the face that lolled so whitely over his arm—the face of a woman, *Nita van Sloan!*

"Nita!" he whispered. "Oh, Nita, you are not dead. You cannot be dead. Nita, my darling...."

As if, even in the depths of hell, she could hear his voice and answer it, Nita stirred faintly. Wentworth had found a washroom and he wet a handkerchief, and bathed Nita's temples.

He tore at her clothing to find the wound and when he found it, tears of happiness streamed unheeded down his face. It was only a bullet burn along the side beneath the arm.

Wentworth joyfully caught Nita up in his arms and fled along the hallway toward the night and safety. His heart chanted a paean of joy. Nita was not lost to him after all. She would never be lost to him again, he swore. She had regained consciousness at last and he stopped for a moment, in the darkness outside the building, held Nita close against his breast.

"Sweetheart," he faltered, "My sweetheart…!"

Nita laughed a little shakily. "Yes, Dick lover, always yours."

Presently, she led him to the car in which she had come and Wentworth drove her off into the night which was kinder than the nights these two had known in recent months. Nita leaned against his shoulder and told him what she knew he wanted to hear, how she had only arrived in Washington when the trouble broke and had followed the ransom representatives when police and other officials had not dared lest they doom the high dignitaries who had been kidnaped—how she had run into Blackmon at the scene….

"He got down on his knees and begged the Spider's pardon for attempting to kill him," Nita told Wentworth. "It seems that after you escaped from him in a hotel and left him in Horace's care, he found a room in which you were sleeping. He stayed in that room all night, trying to get up nerve to kill you, but somehow he couldn't. He had failed twice before and it seemed to him that a voice whispered that he must not. In the morning, the newspapers accused you of kidnaping Tony Horace. He knew you hadn't done that and he began to doubt that you had killed his wife, too. He came to Washington, seeking vengeance for his wife and did as I did, trailed the representatives."

WENTWORTH TURNED from the road into a side lane, switched off engine and lights and turned to Nita. It was cold but there was beginning to be a promise of spring in the air, a dampness that spoke of new budding life, of the birth and happiness of spring. He took Nita in his straining arms.

"Darling," he said slowly. "I want to confess something. I went into this last battle with the intention of getting killed. It is a cowardly thing to admit, but with you gone, things didn't seem...."

Nita put her soft hand across his lips. "Hush, Dick," she whispered. "Everything is all right now. I've proved that the Spider is a different person from Dick Wentworth. He is, you know, Dick, and... Dick, shall I confess, too? I... I was hunting for death, too."

Wentworth was very solemn. "We hunted death... and found happiness. Darling..." He turned toward her, cupped her chin in his hand. "I have done you a great wrong. You were very right and I have been wrong. Because we sought death tonight, let us consider that those old lives are dead. We'll begin life again tomorrow... at the Little Church Around the Corner.

Nita could not hold back the little cry that rose to her lips, "Oh, Dick, you mean...?"

Wentworth said, very tenderly, "I mean, sweetheart, that if you will have me after all these years, we will be married tomorrow."

"And... the Spider is dead?"

"The Spider is dead!" Wentworth's voice was like a bell....

IT WAS not the next day, but two weeks later that Wentworth and Nita went together to the Little Church Around the Corner. Theirs was not an elaborate wedding, but Commissioner Kirkpatrick, who was best man, had been forced to throw police reserves around the church to keep out the crowds. They stood in the smaller chapel, and the smile on Nita's lips was a glorious thing. The rector, in his stole and surplice, had just raised his hand to begin the ceremony when a man's shouting voice sounded in the echoing corridor.

"Kirkpatrick!" he shouted. "Kirkpatrick! They won't let me through...!"

Kirkpatrick turned angrily. Wentworth and Nita glanced curiously back, and an officer in uniform burst through the ranks that opposed him, dashed toward the Commissioner. His face was white, his eyes straining wide.

"The Mayor has been murdered," he shouted. "Murdered with a golden knife shaped like a fly...."

Kirkpatrick turned to Wentworth, grim-faced. "It sounds as if the Fly had come back to life again. He's the crook who almost beat the Spider...."

Wentworth smiled. "I hope the Spider gets him this time," he said calmly. He turned to the rector. "Proceed with the ceremony, please."

Nita's hands were tense on Wentworth's arm, her eyes on his face. It was clear that with his words he had put the life of the Spider away from him as he had promised. Even the return of

187

the Fly, who most among all the men who had opposed him before, Wentworth had admired and dreaded, could not stir him from his determination. There was a rigidity in his jaw that Nita recognized. She whispered his name, and he turned his grave, kind eyes upon her.

"Dick," she said, "It's the Fly."

"So I understand," he said gravely.

"You're... not going, Dick?"

Wentworth's smile became stiff with the hardness of his lips. "I'm not going."

Nita smiled very gently. She put her hands upon his shoulders. "I was wrong, Dick," she said. "I was wrong and you were right. You... will go. You would not be... Richard Wentworth. You would not be... my Dick, if you did not heed their call. Go... and my heart goes with you."

Wentworth hesitated, his hands gripping Nita's arms with paining fierceness.

"Go, Dick!" Nita whispered again.

Wentworth bent swiftly to her lips, whirled to Kirkpatrick. He was not smiling, but there was a hard, eager light in his eyes. The Commissioner shook his head slowly, but he walked beside Wentworth along the aisle, through the crowd and out into the spring sunshine.

NITA SMILED at the rector. "There will be no wedding after all," she said brightly. She turned and walked jauntily up the aisle in the wake of her lover. She held her head very high until she had fled into the darkness of the main chapel itself. Then her head bowed into her hands. There would be no wedding today, or ever, her heart cried. She sobbed, but only once. She dried her tears and walked from the church.

How could she give way to tears? She was the Spider's mate. Soon, she would be fighting by his side again....